"You always seem to be rescuing me."

His arm around her seemed to tighten fractionally. "I can think of worse things."

Her heart was climbing toward her throat. Her gloved hands slid over his, but she didn't know if that was to push his away, or to keep him from pulling away. "Darr—"

His head lowered. His jaw grazed her temple. "Just answer a question for me."

She turned her head, looking up at him, and felt everything inside her grind to a breathless halt. "What?"

"The night of the fire, you said there was no one for us to call for you. No husband. No boyfriend. Was that the truth?"

"Yes." That, at least, was the bald, naked truth.

"Good," he muttered, and pressed his mouth to hers.

Dear Reader,

What is it about Texas that we love? For that matter, what is it about a firefighter? Maybe both just seem larger than life. They call to something in us that longs for wide-open spaces and true heroes.

On the surface, I happen to find that a perfectly lovely image. But beyond the surface are the hearts and the souls of those heroes, and it is there that I find the much more interesting images.

Who is this firefighter who will walk into a burning building without a single hesitation to save another, but is not nearly so brave when it comes to his emotions? Who is this young woman who has walked away from the only life she's known because the fear of the unknown is nowhere near as great as her fear of what she left behind? And how do they impact one another's very existence for the better when their lives collide?

I know I enjoyed finding out as Darr and Bethany shared their world with me, and I hope you'll feel the same.

Happy reading,

Allison

VALENTINE'S
FORTUNE

ALLISON LEIGH

SPECIAL EDITION

Published by Silhouette Books

America's Publisher of Contemporary Romance

Special thanks and acknowledgment to Allison Leigh
for her contribution to the
Fortunes of Texas: Return to Red Rock miniseries.

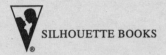 SILHOUETTE BOOKS

ISBN-13: 978-0-373-65433-8
ISBN-10:   0-373-65433-2

Recycling programs
for this product may
not exist in your area.

VALENTINE'S FORTUNE

ALLISON LEIGH

started early by writing a Halloween play that her grade-school class performed. Since then, though her tastes have changed, her love for reading has not. And her writing appetite simply grows more voracious by the day.

She has been a finalist in the RITA® Award and the Holt Medallion contests. But the true highlights of her day as a writer are when she receives word from a reader that they laughed, cried or lost a night of sleep while reading one of her books.

Born in Southern California, Allison has lived in several different cities in four different states. She has been, at one time or another, a cosmetologist, a computer programmer and a secretary. She has recently begun writing full-time after spending nearly a decade as an administrative assistant for a busy neighborhood church, and currently makes her home in Arizona with her family. She loves to hear from her readers, who can write to her at P.O. Box 40772, Mesa, AZ 85274-0772.

For my own Valentine.

Prologue

"Miss?" The deep voice seemed to come at Bethany from a long, hollow distance. "I'm with the Red Rock Fire Department. You're safe now. Just open your eyes."

Her throat hurt. Breathing in made her nose burn. She wanted to sleep. How long had it been since she'd had a decent night's sleep? Since before…before what?

Her brain searched, but all it found was fog. Thick, choking fog.

"Come on now, darlin'. Open your eyes for me."

She was floating in the fog. Was she flying? Someone had told her if she flew in her dreams that meant something good.

A dream. That was it. She was dreaming.

"Dammit, make a hole," the deep voice barked. "She needs air."

She winced. She wanted to shrink away from the harsh command in his voice. Didn't he know she was sleeping?

"Breathe through my mask." The voice was low again. Intimate. "It'll help."

Something covered her face. She pushed at it. Tried to protest. Sucked in oddly sweet air. She turned her head away. "No." The word scraped her raw throat.

"That's it, Miss. Come on back to us. You're doing fine now."

She could follow that voice anywhere. Even up and out of her dreaming fog.

"You're safe now," he coaxed softly. A lover's whisper.

No. That wasn't right. Her lover was…where?

She frowned at the pain inside her head. "No."

"Yes, you are safe. I promise. Just open your eyes. You'll see. Can you tell me your name?"

Bethany. The name sighed through her. *My name is Bethany.*

She jerked, her eyes flying open to stare into the face of the man speaking to her.

Voices. Shouting. Sirens. Smoke. Flashing lights.

It all accosted her in that instant and fear shot through her, making her stiffen. She tried to work her hand to her abdomen, but couldn't seem to manage it. "What?"

"Can you tell me your name?"

Relief was swift, but fleeting. She hadn't said her name. Or if she had, he hadn't heard it. Not over the incredible clamoring confusion surrounding them.

She started to clear her throat. Coughed. What was the name she was using? "Barbara," she finally supplied. Her voice wasn't much more than a croak. Her brain just didn't feel like cooperating. "Burr—" *Not Burdett. Not Burdett.* "Burton." That was her borrowed name. "What happened?"

"Don't worry about a thing now, Barbara. You're safe," was all he said. "I've got you now."

He was carrying her, she realized, and just as quickly she

felt consumed with dizziness. She closed her eyes, but that didn't help. "I feel sick."

The floating, rocking motion ceased. "I'll bet. I'm going to put you on the stretcher now. Just relax."

She opened her eyes again as he settled her on a firm, blessedly steady surface. "What happened?" she asked again. He had streaks on his face. Like war paint. And shoulders wider than a linebacker. He looked armed for battle.

She realized vaguely that a large white van was next to them.

"I almost didn't find you when we were clearing the restaurant." He'd leaned down closer to her and his voice was softer. Impossibly gentle.

Comforting.

She blinked. Rubbed her eyes. Realized that they were watering.

"The smoke was thick in there. You were unconscious," he said. "They're going to take you to the hospital. Just as a precaution. Make sure you're all right."

She didn't want to go to the hospital. She wanted, she wanted…she didn't know what she wanted. "A fire," she said, stupidly. Thickly. Even now, she could see the lick of hungry red lighting the sky beyond the van—an ambulance. And beyond that, a rise of thick, cloying smoke.

Oh, God.

She slid her hand over her abdomen. Please, *please* be all right. "I came for an enchilada."

His teeth flashed. "Afraid you'll have to wait a while for that. Inhaling smoke the way you did can make you pretty woozy," he said.

It wasn't war paint on his face. It was soot. And the armor he wore was a fireman's uniform.

"*You* rescued me?"

"Yes, ma'am." She realized his grin was slightly crooked. "And you're gonna be just fine, Barbara. D'ya have someone you want us to call? Husband? Boyfriend? Who were you with at Red?"

Red. The restaurant. She'd been treating herself to the first meal out she'd had since she'd landed in Red Rock. A woman only turned twenty-five once in her life, right?

"Barbara?"

Her mind was wandering. She knew it. She just couldn't seem to make herself stop. "I'm not married." It seemed to be the only clear thought in her head. "There's no one to call."

"We've got her now, Darr." A woman and another man appeared beside the stretcher and before Bethany could marshal another coherent sentence, they pushed the stretcher and she felt herself slide smoothly into the rear of the white ambulance. The woman followed her.

But Bethany wasn't looking at her.

She was watching the fireman, still standing there.

And then the ambulance doors closed and she wanted to protest, but it was already too late, because she could feel the vehicle begin to move.

The ambulance attendant closed her cool fingers around Bethany's wrist. "What's your name, ma'am?"

Bethany closed her eyes again. In her mind, though, was the firefighter's crooked grin. His deep, gentle voice.

"Barbara." Again, the lie scraped along her raw throat. "Barbara Burton."

Chapter One

Two Weeks Later

"You know you're nuts, right? Might even say you're obsessed. Face it. The woman's gone. Like a lot of folks, she was probably just passing through Red Rock, anyway."

Darr Fortune eyed his brother, Nick, over the lunch counter at SusieMae's. "Thanks for the support."

Nick grinned. "That's why you wanted me to move back here, isn't it? Give my baby bro some ego boosting?"

"Yeah. That was it," Darr agreed drily. He was the youngest of five, it was true, with an entire decade between him and JR, the oldest. But one thing he'd never particularly lacked was ego. A trait shared by his four brothers. "Didn't have a thing to do with the Foundation."

"You just wanted me to put in my time there so *your* conscience would be clear to play around with matches and rescue damsels in distress." Nick flicked the pink message slip that sat on the counter between their empty lunch plates. Around them, SusieMae's buzzed with customers. Most likely because SusieMae's pretty waitresses wore short, sassy little checkered dresses that looked as though they'd been designed by Daisy Mae, herself. "Like the blond babe you've been hunting for since Red went up in smoke."

"I haven't been hunting for her." The denial was weak, and he knew it. So did his brother, considering the way Nick snorted. "I'm only trying to follow up. Make sure she's all right. I *did* pull her out of a burnin' building." He kept his voice light. Not even Nick would know how hard that was.

"Two weeks ago, Darr. And nobody says you're not a hero. Though why you want to go into something that's on fire when everyone else with a lick of sense is trying to get out still escapes me." He pushed a pair of glasses onto his nose and picked up the message slip. "Whoever wrote this ought to be sent back to school. I can't tell the sevens from ones, and is that last number an eight or what?"

"Devaney took the message." Darr slid the message out of his brother's fingers and peered at it himself. He'd been puzzling over the writing ever since he'd found the message tacked to the board outside his quarters at the firehouse. "Except for the street—I think it's Windrose—I can't read the rest of the address he wrote down, either. And Devaney can't remember." The other man was a hell of an engineer, but he was miserable when it came to remembering the details of anything that didn't pertain to a burn. "He couldn't even tell me who called with the address."

It probably hadn't been the hospital, relenting on its confidentiality stance. More likely, it was one of the cabbies Darr had bribed. Hitting it lucky by finding the one who'd actually driven Barbara Burton away from the hospital when she had checked herself out almost as quickly as the ambulance had gotten her there.

"I'm telling you. Obsessed. You ought to put that attention into taking the next promotion exam for captain."

Darr let that pass and Nick picked up his coffee mug, which had gone empty for too long, and gestured toward the waitress behind the counter. "Hey there, sugar. Have some hot stuff any time soon?"

Sugar, more commonly known as Lorena, strolled over and leaned against the lunch counter, giving them both a healthy view of her award-winning cleavage above pink and white checks while she refilled Nick's cup. "This soon enough for you, cutie pie?"

"It is now," Nick toasted her with his cup.

"You want a top-off, Darr?" Lorena barely looked his way. Why would she? Darr was a regular in SusieMae's. Had been since he'd moved to Red Rock from California alone himself, a few years back. She'd learned quickly enough that he wasn't the kind of man she wanted—namely, someone other than a firefighter.

Nick, however, was fresh pickings.

"I'm good, Lorena. Thanks."

"Heard you're working at the Fortune Foundation," Lorena said to Nick. "A financial analyst. Guess little ol' Red Rock must seem pretty tame after Los Angeles."

"Darr got used to it well enough." Nick eyed her, his amusement plain. "And I've always been better at everything than my baby brother."

Lorena glanced at Darr. "Really." Her speculative gaze slid back to Nick's. "I might just have to test that out someday."

"Lorena, order's up," SusieMae barked from the kitchen. *She* did not wear a dress short on length and low on material. A true blessing to the thriving community of Red Rock, Texas.

Lorena straightened up in a leisurely way. "See you later, cutie." She went over to the window and collected her order.

"Maybe Red Rock'll be more entertaining than I thought it would be," Nick mused.

"Oh, Lorena's entertaining all right." Darr pulled out his wallet. "But she doesn't want just a good time. She wants a ring and a baby carriage, too."

"Now, what makes a perfectly attractive woman want to go ruining things that way?" Nick shuddered as he pulled a clip of folded bills from his pocket. "I got it."

Darr tossed enough bills onto the counter to pay for his own meal with a decent tip for Lorena included. The Fortunes might be a wealthy bunch, but he'd always made his own way on his own terms. "I'm not broke." Not that he was earning here what he'd pulled down back in California. But his reasons for coming to Red Rock had much less to do with money than to do with his sanity.

Which Nick figured he'd now lost, anyway, given his futile hunt for the blonde from the fire at Red.

Maybe he's right.

Making certain that Barbara Burton was all right wouldn't erase what had happened with Celia in California.

"Geez." Nick's voice brought Darr back from thoughts of the woman he hadn't been able to save despite his best efforts. "Nobody said you *were* broke. Maybe you'd better go find the blonde, after all. A roll with a pretty woman might make you less touchy. Most folks are happy to get a free meal."

"I'm not looking for a roll." Just a way to sleep at night.

He shoved the message slip into his pocket and grabbed his leather jacket off the empty stool beside them, heading for the door. "Or a free meal."

Nick caught up to him, pulling on his own coat. "Christ, it's cold. This time of year the weather shouldn't be much different from Los Angeles. If I'd wanted to freeze, I could've taken that job in Chicago I was offered last year. Did you see the weather report this morning? They say if the storm veers, it could actually snow here."

"Don't bet on it. I don't care what the weather reports say. It hasn't snowed here in more than twenty years." But they could see their breath, which wasn't at all usual, and the sky looked heavy and gray. "So how *are* things going at the Foundation?"

Nick shrugged, shoving his bare hands into his pockets. "They're fine. Working for a philanthropic outfit is definitely different. Red Rock is different than it used to be, too. Helluva lot bigger." They reached their vehicles—Nick's racy Porsche and Darr's not-so-new black pickup, parked slantwise into the curb in front of the busy diner. "How long are you going to keep hunting for this woman?"

Until I find her. Darr pulled open his truck door. "I'm not hunting."

"Yeah, right. You know there'd be easier chicks to have the hots for than some woman who basically disappeared in the night."

"I don't—"

"Save it." Nick shook his head and pulled open his own door. "Why d'ya think Uncle Patrick wants to meet us out at the Double Crown later? His and Lacey's place in town would be more convenient than Lily's." Lily had been married to their father's and uncle's cousin, Ryan Fortune, and after his death had thrown herself even more into the kind of good works that Ryan had always favored.

"At first I thought it must be something to do with the charity event Lily's hosting at the ranch later this month, but now I don't think so. Patrick wouldn't call in the entire family for a children's picnic. I hope to hell it's not 'cause he's sick or something."

Nick grimaced. It was all too easy remembering when their mother, Molly, had died just two years earlier. Typically though, neither one of them commented on that. "You got the shift off?" was all Nick asked.

"Switched with another guy to get it."

"Dad and the others are taking a car in from the airport, so I could pick you up on my way out there."

Darr shook his head. "I've got some stuff to do first. I'll just see you there."

"Stuff. Like your blonde." Nick shook his head again, as if he wanted to say more, but he refrained, and slid down into his car. "Later."

Darr returned the brief wave and got behind the wheel of his truck. He didn't watch Nick pull out into the moderately busy traffic on the main drag behind him. He was too busy trying to decipher the address Devaney had jotted on the phone message.

Nick was right: Darr was nuts. What else could explain the lengths he'd gone to trying to track *her* down?

Barbara Burton.

His thumb beat against his steering wheel as he waited for a rusted-out station wagon to pass.

It wasn't just her name that stuck in Darr's thoughts.

It was those cornflower-blue eyes of hers.

No, not just blue. Despite the light that night, mutated and muddled by the flashing beacons, by spotlights, by smoke and flames, he'd been able to see that bruising color. The panic in them, followed by relief. Trust. The intimate, soul-wrenching kind of trust that had absolutely nothing to do with sex and everything to do with a basic human need for connection.

That, and the discernible swell of her abdomen that he'd felt when he'd lifted her unconscious and otherwise very slender form, off that smoke-filled restroom floor.

A horn tooted.

He blinked, and shoved the truck into Reverse, backing out into the road, clearing the parking spot for the SUV waiting behind him.

For two weeks, he'd tried to coax and cajole information about Barbara from anyone and everyone who'd had contact with her the night of the fire. The best he'd gotten out of the emergency room had been that she'd left AMA—against medical advice—in a cab. That had led to some greasing of palms at all the cab companies that could conceivably service the community of Red Rock, which was located about twenty miles outside of San Antonio.

His attempts had involved a fair number of cab companies. It had meant a lot of "grease."

Darr probably would have been wiser to let Nick pay for his lunch.

He turned off Main and wound his way through a quieter, modest residential area until he reached Windrose. There, he turned left and began hunting for the first possible combination of house numbers from the message.

Four houses later, he'd netted himself two slammed doors in his face and a third, more kindly shake of a head before the door closed. In his face. The fourth house, he hadn't gotten an answer to his knock at all, but the sight of two motocross bicycles and an abandoned hockey stick in the front yard made him pause.

Barbara Burton had told him that night that she had no husband. And while he strongly suspected that she was pregnant now, she nevertheless looked too young to have children old enough to ride those bikes. Still, he scrawled a note on the back of his business card that he was looking for Barbara Burton and tucked it into the doorframe.

He returned to his truck, and headed back in the other direction. The street narrowed. Well-tended yards grew smaller and then disappeared altogether.

He grimaced when the pavement ended, leaving nothing but scattered gravel and ruts.

In the few years since he'd moved to Red Rock, he'd thought he'd learned every bend in every corner in every street. But he knew for a fact that he'd never been out this way.

He passed a turnoff just before the road started to climb. A lone house sat facing the other street and he followed it, but the address on the mailbox stuck in the weedy yard wasn't remotely close to Devaney's scrawl and he veered around back to the original road. For all he knew when he reached the top of the hill, it would end at exactly nothing, and this would be just one more wasted afternoon looking for a woman who might as well be a ghost.

He crested the hill and a small house came into view.

His boot lifted off the gas and the truck slowed, nearly coming to a stop. In his chest, though, his heart had started pounding. His hands tightened around the steering wheel.

The house—hell, it was more of a cottage, considering its size—sat about fifty yards off the miserable excuse of a road. There was no neatly trimmed, nicely bordered lawn in front of it. Instead, there was cold, bare dirt. Scrubby bushes. The cottage had probably been painted a cheery yellow once, but now it just looked faded and sad, and the open-sided carport next to it seemed to have a tilt. But there was a curl of smoke coming from the chimney, and the rear corner of a car was visible in the listing carport.

So his foot hit the gas again.

Gravel spit from beneath his tires. "Get a grip, Fortune," he muttered, and turned toward the house, heading up a virtually nonexistent driveway.

He parked in front of the cottage and when he got out, the slam of his truck door sounded loud and ungodly intrusive. He looked around. There didn't seem to be a breathing soul anywhere.

It was almost hard to believe he was still in Red Rock.

He exhaled, causing another cloud to ring around his head, and brushed his sweating hands down the front of shirt before pulling up the zipper on his jacket. If this *wasn't* Barbara's house, he was going to tear up that damn message and that would be the end of it.

No more hunting. No more obsessing.

She was a woman with her own life who didn't need complete strangers tracking her down, and finding her wouldn't change the things for him that couldn't be changed.

He rounded his truck and went up the three cracked concrete steps leading to the door and knocked.

No answer.

He knocked again, craning his head back to look at the smoke rising from the chimney. Definitely an active little blaze in the fireplace. But there was still no answer.

He knocked harder. "Hello! Anybody there? I'm with the Red Rock Fire Department," he called out. "I'm looking for Barbara Burton."

* * *

Bethany jumped when the deep voice—oh, it sounded much too familiar—passed easily through the thin door.

She pressed her hand to her heart, willing it to calm. At least it wasn't Lyle. Or worse—her parents.

She hid behind the faded curtain at the front window, and lifted the corner of the thin fabric. Just an inch. Just enough to see the front stoop.

The man standing there was definitely not her father. He wasn't as tall as Lyle, but his shoulders were about a mile wider. She'd never seen her ex-fiancé wear blue jeans—not once in the four years she'd known him—but if she had, she knew the rear view of him in them wouldn't have been as stellar as the one on her porch.

Like a hunting dog scenting its prey, the shaggy dark blond head turned at just that moment, catching her peeking through the curtain.

She jumped back, dropping the curtain back into place.

This time when her heart thudded unsteadily, it wasn't fear that her parents and Lyle had managed to track her down to press her into the marriage that was only designed to benefit them.

The thin door rattled again under the firefighter's firm knock. "Ms. Burton. Answer the door, would you? I'm not here to bother you. Not for long, anyway. I'm just, uh, just doing some follow-up."

She ran her hands down the long sleeves of her oversize fisherman's sweater. Pushed the hem farther down the thighs of her jeans. Cautiously moved around to the door and undid the lock. She pulled the door open as far as the safety latch allowed. She'd installed it herself, miraculously enough. Armed with an instruction booklet from the hardware store and using tools that the kindly manager there had let her borrow.

She eyed the fireman through the two-inch space. "Follow-up?"

He turned his light-blue eyes her way and smiled, causing faint crows' feet to crinkle appealingly into existence. "Yes, ma'am."

Her heart did a squiggly little dance inside her chest. She tightened her grip on the doorknob. "Is that common? I mean, I've never been rescued from a burning building before. I don't know the protocol, I guess."

His head tilted to one side. "It's not unheard of."

Unfortunately, she didn't know what to make of that. But the gust of cold wind blowing in through the crack was enough to jog her into action. "Just a minute." She pushed the door closed again, slid off the safety bolt, and opened it again. "It's freezing out there. Maybe you should come in." He'd saved her life, after all. Leaving him standing out on the porch just seemed impolite.

She felt a vague sense of hysteria. Such a thought could have come out of her mother's all-about-propriety lips.

His head dipped a little as he entered, and a quick vision of him tipping the brim of a cowboy hat in some old-fashioned, courtly gesture flitted through her head.

Her hormones weren't just wreaking havoc with her body. They were doing a number on her imagination, too.

She hurriedly pushed the door shut, feeling the resistance against the gusting wind. But then that left her facing *him*.

He wasn't exactly staring at her, though. No, he was too busy glancing around the modest confines of her simple house.

Home, she corrected mentally. This was her home now. And it was far preferable to the palatial estate she'd grown up in.

"You should turn that screen around in front of your fire," he said after a moment. "It's backwards."

She looked toward the fireplace, feeling foolish. In the six weeks since she'd lived in the cottage, her ability to lay a fire there had improved considerably. For one thing, she'd learned how not to fill the small space with smoke. "I bought the screen second-hand," she admitted, going over to turn it around. The cottage hadn't come with one.

What it had come equipped with was a hopelessly outdated couch upholstered in a hideous orange. A kidney-shaped cocktail table. Spindly-legged dinette set.

Anything else would just have to wait. At this point, and for some time to come, her money was too precious to waste.

She moistened her lips. The silence between them was painfully acute, broken only by the sharp whistle of wind outside and the soft crackling of the burning wood in the fireplace. "I never had a chance to thank you for what you did." She flushed a little. "I'm sorry. Do I call you *officer* or what?"

He shook his head, smiling faintly. "You can just call me Darr." His lashes were ridiculously thick.

And she felt ridiculous for noticing such a detail. He wasn't there as a prospective date, after all—even if she were in the market for such a thing. Which she wasn't.

Besides, he'd already said he was merely following up.

"Would you like something hot to drink…Darr?"

His smile widened. Enough to reveal a faint dimple alongside his sculpted lips. "That would be great."

She quickly looked away and moved over to her small, efficiency kitchen. "C-coffee?"

"Perfect."

It was perfect. And it kept her busy for a few minutes. Minutes that she should have been able to use forming something to say. Instead, she stood there at the minuscule counter, as tongue-tied as she could ever recall being, and focused on the coffee. The smell of it. The blessed act of adding grounds to the small coffeemaker. The spit and sigh of liquid when it streamed hot and fragrant into the glass pot.

Unfortunately, she could only inhale the aroma, since coffee was verboten these days. She finally looked back at him, only to find him standing at the window. He'd pulled aside the faded, floral curtain to look outside. "Do you take sugar? Cream?" Not that she had any cream. But she did have plenty of milk since it had now replaced her beloved coffee.

"Black's fine."

She turned back to her task and pulled a mug from the open shelf that ran the length of the wall above the stove and the sink. Aside from the cupboard next to the refrigerator, the shelf was about the only storage the kitchen afforded. She stood at the counter, watching the coffeepot slowly fill, feeling the tick of every second.

There'd been a time when she could at least carry on a conversation with anyone. Even a handsome stranger.

What had happened to her?

Foolish question, when she knew exactly what had happened. More particularly, *who* had happened.

She yanked the pot out a few moments too early and coffee drips sizzled against the hot plate. She filled his mug and turned to give it to him, only to start at the sight of him standing behind her. Coffee sloshed over the edge of the mug and she sucked in a breath, hastily setting it back down.

He tsked. "I didn't mean to startle you. Better run that under water."

She evidently didn't move quickly enough to suit him,

because he took her wrist, nudging her back the two steps it took to reach her sink, and turned on the ancient faucet.

Air seemed to stop up in her chest as he guided her hand beneath the cool water. She prayed that he couldn't feel the way her pulse had started racing.

"Better?" His voice was soft, brushing against her temple.

She swallowed. Nodded jerkily. "Yes. Thank you."

"Don't thank me. I'm the one who made you jump." He switched off the faucet and gently wrapped the inexpensive tea towel she'd had looped over the oven door handle around her wrist. He blotted away the water and looked at the pinkish mark that still remained on the back of her hand and wrist. His lips compressed. "I don't know what's worse than a burn."

"It hardly stings," she assured. At least she was hardly aware of it when every other nerve in her body was attuned much more acutely to something else.

Him.

She picked up the mug again, refilled it, and handed it to him. "Have a seat."

He walked to the couch. "You're not having any?"

She wiped up the spill with the tea towel and sat on one of the kitchen table chairs. "Keeps me awake at night." Her hands were brushing nervously over her thighs and she tucked her fingers beneath her legs to hide them. "Do you need to fill out a report or something?"

His eyes narrowed over the brim of the mug as he sipped the hot brew. "Report?"

"You know. Follow-up and all that."

"Not exactly."

She felt a fluttering in her abdomen. "Did the hospital give you my address?"

He leaned forward and set the mug on the table in front of him. He'd unzipped his leather jacket and it parted enough for her to see a dark blue T-shirt beneath, with a Maltese cross and "RRFD" printed in white letters on the front. "Something like that."

She tried not to let panic run rampant through her. He'd found Barbara Burton. Not Bethany Burdett. There was no reason to think that Lyle or her parents were any closer to finding her.

"If I'd gotten a phone number for you, I'd have called first. The hospital told me you'd left AMA."

She smiled weakly. Her phone number—"Barbara Burton's" phone number—was unlisted and she certainly hadn't left it with the hospital. She'd only hooked up the phone line because common sense told her that she should, given her situation. "The hospital wanted me to stay for observation. Just…in case. But the doctor told me I was fine, so I came home. It's a lot more affordable sleeping in my own bed than in a hospital one." She didn't know why she was explaining herself to him, but she couldn't seem to stop herself.

Maybe it was those kind eyes of his.

"Insurance?"

She shook her head. "Not yet." But soon.

"I don't mean to pry, but you know there *are* programs."

He meant charitable ones, she knew. Like those administered and funded by the Fortune Foundation where she'd managed to get a job as a receptionist. "I know. But I've just started a new job. I couldn't afford to miss work."

He didn't look entirely convinced. She supposed firefighters with the Red Rock Fire Department were covered with more than adequate health insurance. And truthfully, before she'd escaped from Dallas, she'd never thought about her own need for it because her parents had handled such matters. And after her parents, it would have been Lyle to see to that sort of detail.

Naive. She'd been so painfully naive. Keeping busy with attending the charity balls that *her* family had supported. Picking out the gowns for her ten bridesmaids. Selecting the most suitable china pattern to grace her and Lyle's dining table. And all the while she'd never known the real reason behind Lyle's proposal.

"Where *do* you work?"

She rose and went to the fireplace, and took a split log from the untidy stack of them on the hearth. "The Fortune Foundation." She moved the screen aside long enough to carefully stick the log on the dwindling fire.

"No kidding."

She looked over her shoulder, catching a somewhat bemused look on his face.

"Is that so surprising?" She couldn't think why it would be. *He* didn't know who she really was. What kind of frivolous, useless life she'd led before she'd escaped.

"No. The Foundation employs plenty of folks around here. It just seems kind of ironic."

She brushed her hands together and straightened. "Why?" Lordy, but the man had such a face. She'd been able to tell that even when he'd been streaked with soot and she'd been incapable of coherent thought.

"I've been hunting for you for two weeks," he admitted, still with that faint smile toying around his lips. "And there you were, under our nose all that time."

Hunting? A sliver of unease slid through her. "*Our* nose?"

"The Fortunes," he said easily. "I'm Darr Fortune."

She swallowed. "I see." Which meant he was probably rich as sin and raised in privilege.

Just like Lyle.

"Well." She brushed her hands together again. "As you can see, I haven't suffered any ill effects from the fire. Thanks to you."

She was fine.

More important, the baby she was carrying was fine.

And it was time for this wealthy, privileged, handsome man to go.

Happily, Darr took her hint. "Right." He pushed to his feet and she had the fanciful impression of a deceptively lazy cat rising out of the grass. "Like I promised, I wouldn't take up much of your time." He headed to the door, only to stop and pull something from the inside pocket of his jacket. "If you ever need anything, you just call." He handed her a small white business card.

She took it, excruciatingly aware of how carefully she avoided touching him. The Fire Department insignia embossed on the corner winked up at her. "Lt. Darwin Fortune" was printed in the center. "I'm sure I won't, but thank you."

He nodded and after a hesitation that she wasn't sure if she'd imagined, he reached for the doorknob. "Or you can call even if you don't need anything," he added with a quirk of a smile.

Her mouth ran dry. She didn't know what to say to that and all that came out was an embarrassingly inadequate "Oh."

The quirk twisted a little. "Be sure and keep that fire banked now." He opened the door.

And they both gaped at the wholly unexpected sight of snow.

Chapter Two

"Damn," Darr breathed, disbelieving. He'd never hear the end of this from Nick. "Would you look at that?"

Barbara slid between him and the doorway, peering out. "I didn't think it snowed here!"

He dragged his abruptly diverted attention away from the soft scent of her hair and looked over her head at the strange sight. "It hasn't ever since I've lived here."

She tilted her head, looking up at him, and the impact of those purple-blue eyes of hers was like a blow to his midsection. "How long is that?"

"Close to three years. The forecast earlier said the storm might veer this way, but—" He shook his head, still bemused. Hell, he was a Southern California kid despite the cowboy boots on his feet. Snow wasn't in his vocabulary unless he'd been heading out for a ski trip.

Already a thin layer of white was lacing across the hood

of his truck, only to get snatched away in a swirling gust of wind that seemed to head right through the doorway where they stood.

She shivered and quickly shut the door again, leaning back against it. "So much for forecasts." She brushed her hand through her hair, drawing it away from her smooth forehead. "Maybe you'd better wait until it lets up."

He didn't have to glance at his watch to know he was already cutting things close with the family meeting his uncle Patrick had called. It would take some time to drive out to the Double Crown as it was. And it didn't take a genius to recognize that though Barbara had made the offer for him to stay, she wasn't holding her breath in anticipation that he'd accept.

If anything, she looked nervous at his presence.

Another blast of wind whistled past her window and the bare lightbulb in her kitchen flickered. "Do you have more wood?"

She nodded. "The owners have a stack under the carport that they said I could use if I wanted." She smiled weakly. "I never thought I would be in a situation to *need* it, though. I just liked the scent of a fire in the fireplace. You, um, you don't think the electricity will go out, do you? Everything in here runs on electricity, including the heat."

She plainly hoped he would reassure her that it wouldn't. "Probably better to be safe," he said. "I'll bring in more wood for you just in case. If you've got candles or a lantern—" she pulled a face at that one "—candles, then, or a flashlight, you might put them out somewhere handy."

She moved by him, and he quickly headed out the door. But again the soft, feminine scent of her as she'd brushed past him stuck in his head.

He found the firewood stacked against the side of the house, but few of the logs had been split. He wasted some time looking around for an axe to rectify that, but didn't find one. Not even in the storage bin squatting in front of her twenty-year-old sedan. So he gathered up the pieces that *had* been split and carried them inside, bowing his head against the stinging wind.

One more armload, and he'd made a stack of wood that climbed a reasonable piece up the wall next to the fireplace. "That ought to be enough to keep you warm through the night even if the electricity does fail." She'd need wood in the morning if it did, though, which meant he'd be coming back— with an axe—one way or the other.

Her heart-shaped face seemed to pale a little more. "It's just a little snow. I'm sure it'll stop any minute."

"You're probably right," he agreed, keeping his tone easy. He moved aside the curtain again and looked out. If anything, the sky looked even heavier. Darker. He dropped the curtain again. If he was going to get to the Double Crown, he needed to get moving.

Knowing that didn't alleviate his reluctance over leaving her, though.

She had a small television sitting on one corner of a dresser across from the couch. "You might want to keep that on," he suggested. "Watch for the weather report." The snow was one thing, the plummeting temperature another. She might need to burn the wood even if the electricity held. By the looks of the cottage, he doubted it came equipped with anything other than the most rudimentary heating system.

She'd folded her arms across her chest. "I will." But she made no move toward the television and he couldn't help but wonder if the ancient-looking thing even worked. He also knew that asking if it did would probably just embarrass her. And she'd been embarrassed enough about the fireplace screen.

She had wood, he reasoned inwardly. She'd put out a few thick candles and a box of matches on the table. She had a phone. It was an old rotary-style model; a landline that didn't depend on electricity.

"Would you like more coffee?"

He shook his head. "I really do need to go," he said truthfully.

Her lashes fell. "Thanks for bringing in the wood." Her voice was almost shy.

"No problem. You've got my number."

"Yes."

That reluctance remained heavy inside him, but he went to the door, anyway. His last glance at her before he let himself out into the blowing snow showed that she hadn't moved. Her arms still crossed, her feet still planted.

And he could see the edge of the business card she was still clutching against the sleeve of her thick, oversize sweater.

He let out a breath and made himself move toward the truck. The lacy white layer over it had woven into a full blanket. He got inside the cab, cranked the engine—and the heat. His wipers cut arching swaths through the layer of snow on his windshield as he steered away from the small house. The truck rocked and jolted over the deep ruts. It took no great imagination to know that her old car would have a helluva lot more difficulty maneuvering the near-trenches even if they weren't filling up with snow.

He made it all the way down the hill, past the lone turnoff and her nearest neighbor before he stood on his brakes and pulled out his cell phone.

Nick answered on the third ring. "Should've taken that bet on the snow after all," his brother greeted. "Where are you?"

"Still in town. Tell Patrick I'm not gonna make it."

"No kidding. Well, whatever is going down here can't be

good. Even Aunt Cindy is here, acting like the Queen herself. Lily is looking pained, and that takes some work."

Darr rubbed his forehead. He was hard-pressed to think of a more gracious woman than Lily Fortune. On the other hand, Darr barely knew their father's only sister, Cindy. Aside from the fact that she'd had nothing much to do with the rest of the Fortunes during Darr's lifetime, she was supposedly pretty flamboyant. She'd spent a good amount of time collecting and discarding husbands, and had little contact with the kids she'd produced along the way.

His father and brothers fly in from California, and now his elusive aunt has come to town? Whatever Patrick wanted to meet about *had* to be critical.

More critical than a perfectly capable woman he barely knew.

"Okay. I'm leaving now," he said decisively.

"Wait up. I thought you knew. The roads have been closed. Only way you're going to get out here to the ranch is if you're on a fire truck with the sirens going and the lights flashing."

Darr muttered an oath and flipped on his scanner. It was filled with chatter about the storm. He always kept the scanner on when he was driving, but for once, his preoccupation with Barbara had taken precedence. "I need to check in at the firehouse." For emergency situations, all members of the department were expected to be on call. "Keep your phone on, will you? I want to know what's so all-fire important to Patrick."

"Will do. Any luck deciphering that address?"

Darr didn't want to talk about Barbara. If the department called him in, he wasn't going to be any more good to her than he was to the family out at the ranch. "Yeah."

"And?"

"And nothing. I've gotta run." He didn't wait for Nick's response as he disconnected the call. With his engine idling and his wipers rhythmically doing their best to conquer the snow, he called in to the department, only to be told emphatically by Devaney that the chief wanted everyone to stay put, right where they were. If the department needed him, they'd send out a vehicle to collect him. As it was, the mayor wanted to declare a state of emergency, based on the freak storm.

The problem was that if the department did send a vehicle for him, Darr knew they'd be going to the apartment he rented across town. So he reluctantly gave Devaney Barbara's address instead, and made the man repeat it back, just to be certain he could read his own miserable writing. "It's a friend's place."

"All your friends are firemen," Devaney drawled. "And they don't live way the hell and gone outside of town."

"She's not a firefighter," he said evenly, knowing that tidbit would earn him an immeasurable amount of ribbing, but it couldn't be helped. "Hopefully the charge in my cell will last until the storm passes."

"At least you'll have fun staying warm," Devaney pointed out. "That is, if you remember how all that works since you've barely had a date with a woman since you moved here."

"At least she's a woman." Darr pulled his truck around in a slow turn. "Unlike the sheep you stupidly prefer over Lorena."

Devaney laughed and told Darr what he could do with himself before hanging up on him. Darr dropped his phone on the console and worked his way back up the hill. Even kicking in the four-wheel drive, the truck struggled with the snowy climb. Once he made it, he looked back down the hill. Or what he could see of it, considering the wall of white behind him that seemed to have no beginning or end.

Realizing that if he dawdled much longer he could well lose sight of Barbara's cottage, he gunned across her yard, not even making a pretense of trying to find that rutted driveway.

He aimed toward the porch, but only made it partway before his tires hit a rut that not even his powerful engine could breach. Swearing under his breath at the owners of the cottage for neglecting to grade the drive, he grabbed his phone and the first-aid kit and a heavy-duty flashlight from beneath his seat. He zipped his jacket to the neck and ducked his head into the storm.

By the time he made it up the porch steps, snow was sliding down his collar, and his hands felt numb when he knocked hard on the door. "Ms. Burton?" The wind carried away his voice, but he yelled through the door, anyway. "It's Darr Fortune again."

The wind nearly pushed him through the doorway when it suddenly opened. Barbara scrambled out of the way before he ran into her. "Sorry." He hastily shut the door again, but it still wasn't fast enough to keep snow from blowing in over the threshold.

"That's okay." She looked startled. "Your hair looks icy! What's wrong?"

He dumped his belongings on the end of the couch and shrugged out of his jacket. Compared to the outdoors, the warmth of her cottage felt almost sweltering. "Do you have a towel? I think I'm dripping on your rug."

"I don't think a little water can do more damage to it." But she quickly left the room and returned with an oversize terry cloth towel. "Here."

He swiped it over his head and his wet neck, then tossed it on the threadbare brown rug. Standing on the towel, he managed to pull off his wet boots, and he stepped off the towel to leave them there instead.

When he looked up at her again, her eyes were even wider, running from his stocking feet up to his face and back down again. "It's worse out there than I expected," he prefaced.

Her hand waved toward the TV. She'd turned it on while he'd been gone. It showed a snowy, but decipherable picture. "The newscaster was talking about a state of emergency."

"I heard. The roads have been closed, too."

She swallowed. "For how long? No. Don't answer that. They wouldn't know that yet, would they." It wasn't a question. "You…you'll just have to stay here then."

"I'm sorry."

She shook her head. "There's no reason for you to be. It's not your fault." She looked back at the television. Then toward her nearly nonexistent kitchen. Anywhere, he noticed, but at him. "I don't have a lot of space. Obviously. But I guess we'll manage. Do you want more of that coffee now?"

"That'd be nice. Thanks."

Her smile was small, but looked genuine. She went to the counter and pulled down the same mug he'd used before. While he'd been gone, she'd obviously washed and dried it. The coffee, however, was still in the pot and still hot. Even when he sat down on the couch, he could see the small green power light on the coffeemaker.

In seconds, she returned, handing him the mug.

"Thanks."

"Are you hungry?"

"Had a late lunch."

She looked only slightly relieved as she perched on the seat of the chair. He'd starve before he'd empty her refrigerator of the contents that he suspected might be meager. "Nick and I— my brother, Nick, he works at the Foundation now."

She slanted a shy gaze toward him. "I haven't met him, but I saw the memo announcing when he started there."

"Right. Anyway, we had lunch today at SusieMae's. They make a great steak sandwich."

"I've seen the restaurant but haven't been inside."

"*Restaurant* seems like a fancy name for the place." He kept his tone calm and light. It was plain that it wouldn't take much for Barbara to jump right out of her skin. "But the food *is* good. SusieMae even has enchiladas on the menu," he added. "Never bothered having one there, though, since Red's always been the place to go for good Mexican food."

Her eyebrows crinkled toward each other over the bridge of her straight little nose. "That's nice," she said slowly.

He set his coffee mug on the spindly coffee table. "The night of the fire, you told me you'd just gone there for an enchilada."

"Oh." Her forehead smoothed out again. "I don't remember telling you that."

"Yeah. People say all sorts of things when there's a fire around their ears."

She suddenly looked painfully casual. "What else did I tell you?"

"Nothing much." There were secrets in those blue eyes. He wondered how many of them had to do with the baby he was fairly certain she was carrying. "You were pretty out of it, which is normal. You told me you didn't want us to call anyone for you." No boyfriend. No husband, she'd said.

So where was the baby's father?

"Right. I do remember that." Her hands were twisted together in her lap, and when she realized his gaze had dropped to them, she flattened them. Brushed her palms down the drawn-up sleeves of her thick sweater, as if she were merely pulling them down over her delicately formed wrists because of the cooling room and looked away from him again.

He hid a sigh. If he couldn't get her to relax that skittishness of hers, they were in for a long evening.

He didn't want to think just yet about what they'd do if he was stuck there all night.

Unfortunately, as the gray afternoon light dwindled into darkness and the snow kept falling, Darr figured he'd be finding out soon enough.

Eventually, Barbara turned on a second lamp. There were only two, and mismatched as hell, but they worked, and that's what counted. "I'd better check the heater." She disappeared for a moment down the hall.

He hoped that hall led to a bedroom, but he wasn't confident that it did. From the outside, the cottage had looked no larger than the space that he could see from right where he sat. If there was no separate bedroom, then she slept right here in this room. He had no idea when sofa beds came into production, but the couch looked as old as he was.

He heard her footsteps and he shoved the cushion that he'd started to check beneath back down into place and picked up his coffee mug again. He'd been drawing out the mug's contents, and the brew wasn't even close to lukewarm anymore. "So tell me about your work with the Foundation," he said when she reappeared. "What do you do there?"

"I'm just a receptionist." She tucked her hair behind her ear and for about the millionth time, he noticed the lack of rings on her fingers. "Nothing as important as what your brother—or any of the other Fortunes do."

"Don't kid yourself. People walking in the office over there get to see *you* right off the bat. They're going to want to open their wallets that second."

Her eyes widened, and he realized just how poorly he'd phrased that; as if her mere presence served as an example of the need for charitable donations. "That didn't come out right. I meant that you're just so pretty, people are going to naturally want to hand over cash...hell." He could feel himself flushing and grimaced. "That's not sounding right, either. You can see why I stick to firefighting."

Her lips twitched. "I think there was a compliment in there somewhere, so I'll say thank you, and leave it at that."

"I appreciate that."

Her smile grew a little wider. "How long have you been a firefighter?"

He was a paramedic, too, but wasn't going to belabor the point. "About ten years now." He plucked the RRFD on the front of his T-shirt. "Been with the Red Rock department for nearly three."

"And before that?"

"Southern California. Born and raised there." He tilted the mug her direction. "You?"

She shrugged. "Texas." She didn't elaborate. "I don't know about you, but I'm getting hungry. I'd planned on spaghetti, but I could fix something else if you prefer."

"Spaghetti's pretty much our staff of life in the firehouse," he assured. "Can I help with anything?"

Her eyebrows rose and she gave a wry glance toward the kitchen area. "Yes, you can stay where you are, so I can reach the stove. As you can plainly see, space is in short supply here."

"If it meets your needs, who cares?"

Her gaze flickered for a moment. Another small smile played about her lips as if the comment pleased her. "True enough." She went over to the kitchen area and began pulling items out of the short, old-fashioned refrigerator. "Will you eat a salad?" She held up a head of lettuce.

"I'll eat anything."

"That's good." Her smile turned impish. "Because my

skills in the kitchen aren't likely to ever net me a job in the kitchen at Red."

"Until the restaurant opens up again, nobody's doing much of anything in the kitchen over there."

"I read in the newspaper that the cause was still under investigation?"

"Yes." The initial presumption of it being a grease fire had been loudly contested by the owner. The duration of the subsequent investigation suggested that José had been right. "They'll probably issue a public statement when the investigation is complete. Should be any day now."

"You can't talk about the details," she surmised.

"Even if I knew them."

"When do you think they'll be able to open again?"

"Not soon enough for José Mendoza. He's the owner. Don't worry, though. You'll be having enchiladas there again before you know it."

She actually laughed softly, and her smile widened enough to show the perfect fine edge of her white teeth. "I'll sleep better tonight, knowing that." She turned away to face the counter and fortunately missed the hard swallow that Darr had to make.

He'd never met a woman before who could make him stop breathing with a simple smile.

He ran his hand down his face. "Your bathroom?"

"Oh. Down the hall." Without taking her attention from what she was doing, she pointed the tip of her knife over her shoulder.

There'd been no other location it could be—other than an outhouse. It also gave him an excuse to see if there was a minuscule bedroom hidden beyond the short hall, too.

There wasn't.

He looked at his reflection in the mirrored medicine cabinet hanging on the wall over a chipped, but shiny clean pedestal sink.

Nick was right. He was nuts.

The bathroom was as small and spare as the rest of the place, particularly with a stacked washer and dryer taking up one corner, but she'd hung a cheerful striped shower curtain on the circular rod above the miniscule bathtub, and stacked matching towels on the iron shelf hanging on the wall. He left the bathroom behind and passed the bare hallway walls again.

There were no personal items around the house at all. No photographs. No dust collectors, as his mother used to call the knickknacks that she'd liked having around their house when he'd been growing up.

His apartment was mostly just a place for him to sleep when he wasn't on duty, but even *he* had some stuff on his walls. His shelves. Maybe they were only ball caps from his favorite teams and a mishmash of photographs—mostly ones his mom had framed and given him—but they were still his.

Barbara seemed to have nothing.

The picture on the television was even snowier than it had been earlier, and he fiddled with the rabbit ears protruding from the back with no results.

"It's hooked up to that converter thing for the new digital signals, but I still only get a few channels," she told him, sounding apologetic.

He just wanted to see any weather report but, at the moment, the only thing he found was a decade-old sitcom, a public television telethon and a reality show. "I hardly ever turn on the TV at my place." He gave up on the limited selection and pulled out one of the chairs at the dinette table. "There's a huge flat screen over at the firehouse that gets plenty of use, though."

She leaned over and pulled a big pot out of the lower cupboard and straightened. He saw her face pale and she braced her palm against the counter, shoving the pot with a clatter onto the stove.

He made it to her in little more than a step, catching her shoulders. "Are you all right?"

"Fine." Her fingers fluttered against her forehead for a minute. "I just straightened too quickly."

"Here." He nudged her toward the chair he'd just vacated. "Sit."

"I'm really fine," she protested, but she sat, anyway.

"Head rush." He filled the pot in the sink and set it on the burner, cranking it to high. "Is there a cover for this thing?"

She pointed to the low cabinet and he pulled out the lid, dropping it on top of the pot. She'd already set out a package of dried spaghetti and a jar of sauce, and the salad was sitting in a large wooden bowl, topped with mangled tomatoes and jagged shards of carrots. He took the salad to the table. "Start on that while the water boils."

"I'm *fine*."

He grimaced. "And stubborn, too."

She gave a disbelieving snort. "If you knew me, you'd know how far off the mark you are."

"Then eat some salad. You've already said you were hungry." He went to the pot, peeked under the lid. The water was just starting to ripple. He dropped the lid back in place. "What about salad dressing?"

"In the refrigerator door."

He pulled on the V-shaped handle. "I haven't seen a fridge like this since I was a kid. I think my grandparents had one like it."

"It's a little old," she allowed mildly.

"It's probably an antique," he murmured. Ancient or not,

the inside was considerably better stocked than he'd expected. She had a liking for fresh vegetables and fruit, and mostly lean meats. "Which dressing?"

"The vinaigrette."

He pulled the bottle out and took it to the table. She still hadn't served herself any salad, and he unceremoniously dumped a good helping on one side of her plate. "Here." He handed her the dressing.

"Are you sure I can manage?" She took the bottle and shook it, looking oddly peeved. "I *can* decide a few things for myself. Like whether I want salad this very minute."

"I'm sure you can decide. And if you want to pass out the next time you stand up, feel free."

She flipped off the bottle top and sprinkled the vinaigrette over the lettuce leaves. "You're just panicked by the idea of having to pick me up off the floor again."

"It takes a lot more than that to panic me," he assured her drily. The water was finally boiling, and he dumped a big handful of spaghetti into the pot. "Do you want me to add salt to the water?"

"I don't add it. Trying to cut down on sodium, too."

No caffeine. No salt. Combined with the items in her fridge and the distinctive bottle of vitamins on her shelf, she was probably an obstetrician's dream.

She had a clear glass mason jar that held cooking utensils sitting on the counter next to the two-burner stove, and he pulled out the largest wooden spoon and gave the spaghetti a stir. He glanced at her, only to find her watching him.

"You seem pretty comfortable in a kitchen." The idea seemed to surprise her. "Even one as dinky as mine."

"We all switch off with kitchen duty at the department." He grinned. "Some days the results are better 'n others."

"Which type of day would you fall into?"

"Better, of course." He slid a piece of spaghetti off the spoon, bit it in half and deemed it done.

She smiled and turned her attention back to her salad. "Why would I have thought anything else?"

He was glad to see that now she'd begun on the salad, it was steadily disappearing from her plate. He drained the spaghetti, tossed the sauce over it right in the pot and carried it to the table. He pulled out the chair opposite Barbara, sat, and reached for the salad. "My mom was a great cook. She did her best to teach me and my brothers how to find our way around a kitchen. It probably wasn't as effective as she'd have liked. But I can boil water and make a mean turkey sandwich."

She still looked amused. "How many brothers do you have?"

"Four. No sisters. How my mom put up with all of us is anyone's guess. You?"

She reached for the spaghetti and scooped some onto her plate. "One brother. One sister." She made a face. "I'm the baby by ten years."

"I'm the youngest, too, but there's only ten years between the entire lot of us."

She twirled her fork through the spaghetti. "Are you the only firefighter?"

"Yeah. The middle one, Jeremy, is a doctor in northern California, but the rest keep more to the number-side of business."

"Bailey—my brother—is a doctor," she surprised him by offering. "Julia's a lawyer. They're the brilliant ones." She swallowed a mouthful of spaghetti, delicately sucking in the tail of a noodle and unknowingly sending a blast of heat right down to his gut. Fortunately, her attention was on her plate. "They're both married, but they are *all* about their careers.

And then there's me," she added after a moment. "Receptionist extraordinaire."

The world needed receptionists, too, he figured. Just like
it needed guys like him. "Is there something else you'd
rather be doing?"

Her gaze lifted and collided with his. "Until lately, I've
never really thought about it," she admitted, then just as
quickly flushed and looked down again, seeming to focus
hard on her plate. "Sorry. You don't want to hear about that.
It's hardly interesting dinner conversation."

"Barbara." His voice was quiet. It was all he could do to
keep from reaching out and touching her hand. "Look at me."
He waited until she finally lifted her lashes again and he could
see those striking pools of blue. "Don't you get it? Everything
about you is interesting to me."

She stared back at him. Finally set down her fork and
moistened her lips. "E-even the fact that I'm pregnant?"

Chapter Three

Bethany couldn't believe that the words came out of her mouth.

"I wondered," he said, and shoved a hefty bite of spaghetti into his mouth.

He didn't seem in the least bit shocked. Instead, he was watching her with that steady, utterly calm and capable expression that she'd already come to identify with him.

"You...did? How? Why?" She narrowed her eyes and poked her fork in the air. "Did the hospital tell you?"

"The hospital wouldn't tell me diddly-squat about you, other than that you'd left AMA in a cab."

"Then how did you find me?"

"Cab drivers are a little freer with information about where they deliver their fares than hospitals are with the identity of their patients."

"I should hope so," she muttered and tried to remember how many cabs she'd used since she'd hightailed it out of

Dallas in a semi driven by a portly old man who'd reminded her of her grandfather. Most of the cabs, though, had been in San Antonio, before she'd found herself a car to buy and backtracked twenty miles to settle in Red Rock.

What was the likelihood of her parents or Lyle tracking her down through them? She'd always used cash and had avoided using the same company more than once.

If they had, she'd know it by now. At least that's what she told herself.

There was no reason to panic. *They* weren't here. Darr was.

"How far along are you?"

"Five months." She dropped her fork on her plate and propped her elbows inelegantly on the tabletop. "What *is* it about you that makes people tell you things they have no intention of talking about?"

"I'm a firefighter. People trust us."

She wished it were only that simple. But she feared it wasn't.

"I was a bartender for a while, too," he went on easily, as if there were nothing at all out of the ordinary in their conversation. "Back in my college days. Heard things then that would curl your hair tighter than a corkscrew. Saw things." He shook his head. "Nothing like when I joined the department in Los Angeles, but still. People are crazy." His lips twisted and he looked ironic for a moment. "That's a fact."

She toyed with her fork, watching him. He wasn't exactly handsome. Not in the classical sense, as Lyle was. But there was something far more appealing in Darr's masculine good looks. Something strong. Steady.

Comforting.

And she ought to know better than to let herself get sucked into the lure.

For the first time in her life, she was standing on her own two feet. It felt strange. And scary.

But infinitely better than the life she'd left behind when the only decisions she'd ever made for herself were which shoes best matched which outfit.

Darr was making a serious dent in his helping of spaghetti while she'd had barely more than a few bites.

She twirled her fork through the noodles more intentionally. If he wondered where the father of her baby was, he hid it very well.

She reasoned that asking about Darr might be a way to stem her runaway tongue before she started blabbing about that, too. "What made you want to be a firefighter?"

"Studying finance and economics in college," he said wryly. "It was pretty evident to everyone that I was *not* going to be joining my old man's firm. Fortune Forecasting."

She'd heard of the West Coast firm. Rather, she'd heard her father *talk* about the firm. Probably at one of the endless cocktail parties she'd attended at his behest. "Seems a big jump from balance sheets and marketplace trends to fire hoses."

"Not so big. I wanted to join the academy as soon as I was old enough. He didn't agree. Thanks to my mom's efforts, we compromised. I ended up with the degree he wanted, but got the career that mattered to me. Everyone was happy."

She wished she could say the same about the difference of opinion she'd had with her own parents. But the only way *they'd* be happy was if she shackled herself to Lyle.

And that, she simply would not, *could* not do.

Before she'd come to her senses, she'd wasted far too much time thinking otherwise.

"Do your parents live in California?"

"My mother passed away a few years ago. But my dad still

lives there. He's in Red Rock right now, though." He nudged his empty plate away. "Half the Fortune family is here right now. Just one big happy family reunion."

She noted his faint grimace. To her, he didn't look all that happy about it.

So she switched topics entirely.

"I have cookies if you'd like some dessert. Just store-bought, I'm afraid, but—" She broke off when he lifted his hand, shaking his head.

"Don't knock store-bought cookies." His grimace had been replaced again by that faintly wry grin of his. "Another staple at the firehouse. But I'll pass. Thanks."

Even though she felt keenly on display still eating when he'd already finished, she made herself take several more bites of spaghetti before allowing herself the luxury of pushing back from the table. But before she could reach for his plate, he rose, too, and neatly slipped her plate out of her hands. "Go on and relax. I'll take care of this."

"You've already done too much," she protested. "You practically made the entire meal."

He rolled his eyes. "Boiled some noodles. That's serious effort. Go on. Put your feet up. Isn't that what pregnant women are supposed to do?"

She pressed her lips together for a long moment. But really, what was the point in fighting? There wasn't room for them both to maneuver around the kitchen area. And he looked firmly planted where he stood, as if he would bodily block her from trying to take care of the simple housekeeping tasks if she'd tried. "Do you always get your way?" she finally asked.

His lips tilted crookedly. "On occasion."

That odd squiggle slid through her again. The man was way

too attractive for her peace of mind. "I'll see if there's some news about the storm on the television."

He smiled faintly and she had the embarrassing sense that he knew exactly what kind of effect he had on her. The same kind of effect he probably had on every woman younger than ninety.

She tugged her hair away from her too-warm face and turned her back on him as she flipped the ancient dial-style switch on the television, running through her three channels. In all the time that she'd spent alone in this excruciatingly modest little house, she'd never before wished so strongly that she'd used some of her precious nest egg to invest in a decent television.

She'd have had plenty of cash if she dared to access the trust fund left to her by her grandparents. But she knew her parents would be watching for withdrawals and would find her the moment she transferred any money.

So she'd had to make do with what she had.

As it was, she didn't know what she and Darr were going to do to pass the rest of the evening. It might have fallen into utter darkness outside the windows of the house, but that didn't mean they were anywhere near bedtime yet.

At the mere thought of *that*, her gaze slid guiltily to the sofa bed.

It would be wide enough to accommodate the both of them. If there was very little space between them.

Heat streaked through her and she pulled her focus right back to the safety of the television and its grainy picture. "Darr." She called him and turned up the volume. "The news is on."

He walked over to stand beside her in front of the television. "Sit," he told her again as the local newscaster talked about the balmy weather on the West Coast.

"Bossy," she murmured, but sat on the edge of the side chair.

"That's what gets my job done."

"You weren't bossy the night of the fire," she countered. That night was a jumble of memories, but at least one thing was clear—just how cajoling his voice had been, calling her back to consciousness.

The weather report turned local then, and they both fell silent to watch. Two minutes later, if Bethany had harbored any hopes that Darr would be heading out any time soon, they were firmly dashed with the news that there was another storm front on the heels of the one that had already hit Red Rock.

She didn't know whether to be relieved or disturbed that they would be facing the weather together.

She could not read Darr's expression, as he turned the volume back down when the news slid from weather into sports. He looked as calm and composed as ever.

"That's that," was all he said before returning to the kitchen. Without looking at her, he flipped on the faucet and squirted liquid dishwashing soap into the sink. "Don't look so worried, Barbara. I'll bed down on the floor."

"I—I wasn't worried," she protested automatically, even though it was an outright lie. What worried her, though, was not fearing that he'd expect to find some space on her only bed, but the fact that she wasn't simply appalled by the very idea of it.

She'd been a virgin when she'd become involved with Lyle. Even then, it had been over a year before she'd shared his bed. She'd known Darr, what? Two weeks, if she counted the night of the fire.

All she could seem to think about was the combustible combination of Darr and a bed.

Pregnancy hormones?

Or him?

"I'm, um, I'm going to take a shower," she announced abruptly. "While I can be certain there is electricity to keep the water hot." She didn't wait to see what, if any, reaction he gave, and hurried down the hall, closing herself safely behind the bathroom door.

She flipped on the water, running only the cold so as not to waste the hot while she sat on the closed lid of the commode, her face buried in her hands.

Hormones or whatever, she needed to get hold of herself, and fast. Darr Fortune—moneyed or not—showed all the makings of a perfectly decent man.

He could say everything about her was interesting, but she felt certain that the last thing he needed was a pregnant, runaway bride throwing herself at him.

The second Darr heard the bathroom door close, he braced his hands on the edge of the sink, bowed his head and let out a long, deep breath. He heard the water turn on in there, and ordered himself to stop imagining her shedding her jeans and that all-enveloping sweater; and clothing herself, instead, in hot, streaming water.

There were a lot more pressing matters that should be concerning him.

Like what the hell was going on over at the Double Crown.

Like whether the electricity here in Barbara's dinky house would hold.

Like how deep the snow was, and what the second storm front would bring, and if they were going to have to actually shovel out, as the news had warned people to be prepared to do.

He heard the faint, metallic jangle of the shower curtain being pulled across the shower rod, and his damnable brain went right back into that small bathroom with Barbara.

Annoyed with himself, he yanked the plug from the drain, letting out the water, and rinsed the last of the soapsuds from the dishes.

Was she a washcloth and bar-of-soap kind of girl, or did she like those puffy wadded-up net things that turned a squirt of soap into a mountain of lather?

God. He was a head case.

If he had been half as infatuated with Celia, things would have turned out a whole lot differently. But then, he'd have stayed in L.A., likely married to a woman he didn't love who was carrying another man's child, and it would have been someone else who'd have carried Barbara out of that burning restaurant.

He snatched up the dish towel and dried the big pot and the dishes, sticking them back in their spots on the open shelves. Then, with the kitchen restored to order, he went to the television and turned up the volume again, as if it could drown out the steady hiss of the shower running.

It didn't.

He threw himself down on the couch, only to get right back up again and move, instead, to the chair. He pulled out his cell phone and dialed Nick, but only reached his brother's voice mail. He disconnected, not bothering to leave a message.

He knew that Nick would call when there was something to report.

The shower was still running.

Swearing under his breath at himself, he yanked on his boots and jacket. Then, with the flashlight from his truck in hand, he went outside, where the wind had died down to an occasional gust. The air was still cold, though, and did a reasonable job of freezing through his jacket *and* the heat pooling in his guts.

She had a utilitarian porch bug light that cast just enough of a yellow tint to see the snow piled on the steps. He scraped his boot along the risers to clear the worst of it away as he stepped down them, and played the strong flashlight beam over the area beyond.

The snow was still falling, but instead of the deluge of white that it had been earlier, now it was just a smattering of flakes, catching like firefly glints in the light of the flashlight. He headed around the house to the carport and stepped back far enough to shine his light over the roof. Visibility wasn't the best, but he didn't think the weight of the snow had worsened its uneven cant.

Once things got back to normal, he'd see about getting someone out there to shore up the supporting posts.

He trudged back in front of the house again, where the snow easily reached the top of his boots. Several yards off, his truck was nothing more than a hulking mound of white. He didn't bother wading his way closer.

He could only imagine the chaos all this snow was causing the rest of Red Rock.

He looked up at the sky. No stars to speak of and a snowflake that landed in his eye. He wiped it away and went back inside, only to catch Barbara standing in the center of the living area.

At his entrance, the uneasiness cleared from her face. "I just went outside to check around," he told her. Had she really thought he'd leave her alone now, despite the conditions?

Her fingers flexed around the wide white collar of the velvety-looking robe that covered her right to her toes. "Is it still very bad out?"

"Snow seems to be letting up, but there's a good foot of it on the ground out front." Except for the occasional one he'd given his mother as a gift, he was no particular judge of women's robes. But the one Barbara was wearing looked expensive. Luxurious and so perfectly fitted it might have been made just for her.

It also seemed highly incongruous, considering her exceedingly modest surroundings.

He reminded himself that it was none of his business how she'd come to own a robe like that. Wasn't it bad enough that he'd stuck his nose into her business as much as he had?

He pulled off his jacket and his boots again, leaving them once more by the door. "It's going to take some shoveling to clear the way to the road," he said. "And that road's either going to need plowing, or a whole lot of sunshine and warmth to make it drivable."

She nibbled her lip. "I don't even have a regular shovel, much less a snow shovel."

"We'll figure out something." The town might be short of snow equipment, but that didn't mean there was none at all. And while he knew the emergency protocols would be in place by now, he also knew those measures would first be focused on ensuring that basic services were available for those experiencing true emergencies.

Aside from being cut off from the rest of the town, they had water and were warm, dry and well sheltered.

"Do you think we'll be back to normal by Monday?"

Reassuring people was second nature to him, and it was more than plain that reassurance was what she wanted. But the circumstances were extremely unusual. "Hopefully," he said. "Depends on what that second storm front decides to do. Don't worry about the Foundation office, though. If you can't get there, there're a lot of other people who won't be able to get there, either."

She didn't look particularly comforted by that, though she

did let up on the death grip she had on her robe. "I put out clean towels for you," she said. "For when—whenever you want to use them. I don't have a spare toothbrush, I'm afraid."

"Nobody expects you to turn your home into a hotel," he assured. "I'll be fine. And if you're tired, you can say so. Like I said earlier, I'll pitch camp on the floor."

"You're being very accommodating."

"I think that should be my line. You ended up with a guest you never invited."

She lifted her hands to either side, like scales. "Let's see. I give you a floor to sleep on." One hand dipped slightly. "You save my life." She leaned over with the other hand nearly to the floor. "I think I should be telling *you* to take the bed."

"Don't even try," he warned drily.

"Well." She straightened and brushed her hands together. Toyed with the silky white sash tied around her waist—which was still narrow despite her pregnancy. "As it happens, I am a little tired." She shrugged her shoulders. "It seems like I'm tired most of the time these days."

Celia had been tired 24/7. "You're growing a baby in there," he said, reminding himself to focus on the present. "Gotta take some energy to do that."

She pressed her hand flat against her abdomen. Only then was it obvious that there was indeed a distinct baby bump beneath that rich-looking fabric. "You're the only person in Red Rock I've told. And it turns out you already knew." She suddenly fixed her gaze on him. "If the hospital didn't tell you, how *did* you know?"

"I carried you out of the restaurant."

Great, Bethany thought with a wince. "If I'm that much of a whale already, goodness only knows how huge I'll be when the baby is actually due."

"Honey, you're a far cry from a whale. But you're small. And slender. And I'm a paramedic. I'm trained to notice details. Even if it hadn't been for the way you were holding your hands just like you are now." He nodded toward her, and she realized that her hands were still pressed protectively around the swell of her baby. "Don't worry," he added. "I wasn't feeling you up or anything on the floor in Red."

Her cheeks went hot. "I didn't think anything of the sort!"

"Then stop fretting," he said. "Please. Does this couch pull out, or what?"

"It pulls out."

"Okay. Here." He handed her the first-aid kit that was still sitting on the couch. "Put that down somewhere."

"I'll bet you were a Boy Scout, too," she murmured, setting the large plastic case aside while he lifted the two narrow cushions off the couch to reveal the mechanism beneath. "Be careful. It wants to stick a little. I've smashed a finger or two trying to pull it out."

He grabbed the metal bar and yanked on it, unfolding the bed with absolutely none of the difficulty that she struggled with every night. The thin mattress unfolded, too, and landed on the frame with a soft plop that made the sheets that she left on the bed flutter wildly.

She pulled the thick, tie-dyed comforter that she'd found on the clearance rack at a discount store in San Antonio out of the hall closet. "Here." She handed it to him. "You can use this. Hopefully it'll be enough to keep you warm."

"What about you?"

She reached into the closet again and pulled out another blanket as well as her two pillows, one of which she handed to him. "I don't have a spare pillowcase for you, I'm afraid. But I did laundry just a few days ago."

"I think I'll live," he said gently, with only a hint of amusement. "Barbara, I'm used to sleeping in quarters that most closely resemble a coat closet with a cot inside. I'll be fine."

She smiled weakly. Every time he called her Barbara, she felt a pang of guilt. That's what she got for lying. "The couch cushions would probably be a little softer to sleep on than just the carpet."

With the couch unfolded into a bed that ran sideways, barely two feet away from the fireplace, it was readily apparent that there were few options over which stretch of carpet would hold him for the night. Sleeping at the foot of the bed would leave either his head or his feet running down the short hallway. The other option put him directly in front of the refrigerator and stove.

She wasn't particularly surprised when he tossed the couch cushions in front of the fridge and dropped the comforter on top of them.

Feeling painfully self-conscious, she straightened the rumpled sheets on the thin mattress, and spread out the blanket on top like someone who really was just as tired as she'd claimed to be. Without looking at him, she pulled off her robe and quickly slid beneath the bedding.

When she'd escaped Dallas, she'd left with not much more than a wad of cash from her ATM, which she was still carefully hoarding, and the clothes on her back.

That, of course, had happened to be a designer wedding gown and her grandmother's pearls. The gown, though, had at least proved to be useful in the end. It had netted her enough cash to buy the old car sitting under the carport.

The only other thing that Bethany had taken with her from Dallas had been the suitcase that had already been packed for the honeymoon. She'd been able to snatch it before the chauffeur loaded it into the trunk of the limousine that was to have brought her to the church. She'd traded a good portion of *its* contents in a secondhand store in San Antonio for pots and pans, dishes, the linens they were using right this minute, and nearly everything inside the bathroom except the fixtures that had come with the place.

Now, rather than the filmy white peignoirs that her mother had deemed suitable for a new bride, which were presently stuffed in the bottom drawer of the bureau below the television along with the pearls she couldn't bear to sell, Bethany had chosen instead to wear the thick, serviceable flannel pajamas she'd bought at the same place as the comforter. She was more thoroughly covered than she was even during the day, but there still seemed something painfully intimate about wearing them while climbing into bed with Darr just a few feet away.

Then she made the mistake of sneaking a look toward him as she reached over to turn off the lamp on the little table between the couch and the chair.

He'd pulled off his dark blue T-shirt to reveal a white one that clung a whole lot more to his shoulders.

His very broad, well-muscled shoulders.

She swallowed hard and quickly snapped off the light. "Do you want me to leave on the other lamp?"

"I'll get it." He crossed to the dresser where the TV and the lamp were. "What about the television?"

She often left it on at night. Silly, she knew, but it was some small bit of noise against the utter quiet that, at night, underscored just how alone she was. "It doesn't matter."

He switched off the lamp, but left the television on, the volume turned low so that it gave off only a low murmur of noise. "I'll shut it off after the news. Are you warm enough?"

Beneath the blanket, she curled her toes inside her thick socks. If anything, she was too warm. But that condition had little to do with the temperature inside the house. "Plenty."

"G'night then, Barbara."

My name is Bethany.

She closed her eyes and pulled the blanket nearly to her nose. It made her feel slightly more invisible, but not in the least bit less guilty. "Good night, Darr."

She could hear him moving around as he settled. Heard a faint jingle that she belatedly realized was probably his belt buckle and had to brace against the torrent of images her imagination conjured up over *that.*

And then, all was silent except for the low drone of the television and the occasional gust of wind that rattled the thin windowpane and door.

She lay there, counting off the beats of her heart, then finally pushed herself up on her elbow. With the bluish light from the small television and the warm flicker from the fireplace, she could easily make out the shape of him on the floor, buried under the comforter. "Darr?"

He didn't move. "Yeah?"

"I'm glad you're here," she admitted softly.

He was silent a long moment. "Me, too."

Chapter Four

The next time Bethany opened her eyes, daylight was shining through the curtains and she could hear the distinctive sound of water running in the bathroom.

Darr was taking a shower.

She unwound herself from the blankets, only to pause when she realized he'd spread the comforter on top of her while she'd slept.

The couch cushions that had been his bed were stacked next to the door, with the pillow he'd used sitting on top.

She climbed off the bed and nearly winced at the chilly air that accosted her. Pulling on her robe helped only a little, and she quickly checked the thermostat situated on the wall by the bathroom door. The furnace was running, but the temperature was well below what it should have been.

The running water stopped, and she nearly skipped her way over to the kitchen where Darr had already put on a pot of coffee.

He'd also found her store of herbal tea bags. One was un-wrapped and waiting inside a mug, and on the stove a saucepan was filled with water. He'd obviously heated it for her tea.

Something inside her chest squeezed and she carefully poured the steaming water into the mug and took it to the table. She'd had all manner of beverages and meals prepared for her during her life. Always by a paid staff person.

This was distinctly different.

By the time Darr emerged from the bathroom, she thought she had her silly emotions back in hand as she leisurely sipped the piping-hot tea.

That was until he padded out of the bathroom wearing nothing but his jeans and one of her blue-and-yellow-striped towels looped around his neck.

She dragged her eyes from the most perfectly masculine chest she'd ever seen in her life and took too hasty a sip, nearly choking as it burned down her throat.

"You're awake." He stopped at the coffeepot and took down the mug from the shelf. "I tried to be quiet."

"You were," she managed. She coughed a little, hoping her face wasn't as red as it felt, and lifted her cup again. "I didn't hear you at all. Thanks for the tea."

"Just boiling more water." Leaning one hip against the counter, he turned to face her. His gaze narrowed slightly over the brim of his coffee mug as he drank. "The electricity went off in the night. It came on a few hours ago, but it's been cutting in and out ever since. I decided I'd better make quick use of it while it was on. Shower wasn't entirely cold."

"I didn't even notice the power had been off." She couldn't believe she'd slept so soundly with him there.

Or, maybe she *could* believe it, which was all the more impossible.

"That's why it's so cold in here." He lifted one end of the towel to run it over his wet head. The muscles in his sinewy arms flexed from the cords in his wrist and right on up to his shoulder.

She barely kept herself from chugging another gulp of too-hot tea.

"I turned the furnace up as high as it would go," he continued, blessedly oblivious to her embarrassingly juvenile reaction to his ungodly beautiful torso. "Well…damn." His gaze went to the ceiling as the furnace clicked off with an ominous pop. "There it goes again."

She looked at the coffeemaker. The power light had gone out. "At least you made the coffee in the nick of time." Her mouth fairly watered just from the aroma of it.

Or maybe her mouth was watering because of him.

Either way, the source was something she needed to stay away from.

He rubbed the towel over his chest. "D'you know if there's an axe around here?"

"I have no idea." Focusing her brain on something other than him took an embarrassingly monumental effort. "If, uh, if there is, I think it would be in the storage chest outside."

"I looked yesterday. There wasn't one."

She barely heard him.

Lyle had been an avid swimmer. He played tennis and golf and a host of sports he considered advantageous in the business world. He'd been tall, wealthy and meticulously groomed. Right down to a waxed-smooth chest that didn't hold a candle to what was on display three feet from her nose.

She exhaled carefully and nonchalantly moved away from the table and the overwhelming appeal of the dark hair swirling across Darr's hard chest.

What had they been discussing?

Wood. Axe. Right.

"I don't know where else one would be then," she told him. "The only things the owners left inside were the furniture and a few board games in the hall closet." She lifted the curtain away from the window and looked out, squinting against the reflection of light from an ocean of glistening snow. "Have you *looked* out there?"

He joined her at the window and looked out. "Yeah. This'll be one for the record books all right." His arm barely grazed hers as he turned from the sight. "I know this will probably sound kind of strange, but do you have a pair of socks that I can use?"

"Oh. Sure." She blinked. His bare feet were considerably larger than hers. "Well, we can try." She went to the dresser and pulled open the top drawer, rummaging through the meager contents before pulling out a pair identical to the ones she was wearing. "They're polka-dotted," she stated the obvious.

"And pink," he observed, grinning crookedly. "But they'll do." He sat down on the arm of the couch and pulled them on. On her, the stockings reached nearly to her knee. On him, the fuzzy cotton barely covered his muscular calves. He followed up with his own white socks, then pushed his feet down into his somewhat battered-looking cowboy boots and yanked the hem of his jeans back in place.

"I have a few extra T-shirts," she offered. She felt hot inside. "I bought them with the baby in mind." She held her hands out beyond her expanding middle. "Men's size large." So far she'd only slept in them. She went back to the drawer and pulled one out. "It'll still probably be too tight, but it's clean." It was also plain and white.

"The more layers, the better." He took it from her and worked it over his head, then pulled it down over his chest. As she'd expected, the cotton knit strained at the seams. It also lovingly outlined every rippling line of his torso, from the hard points of his nipples to where the fabric stopped short midway down his six-pack abdomen. "Got another one?"

She blindly grabbed and mercifully came out with another T-shirt and not one of her lacy bras that in the past month had become increasingly snug. "Here."

"Thanks." He pulled it on over the first, followed up with his own undershirt, and then the blue fire department shirt.

When he picked up his jacket, her stupefied brain kicked into gear. He needed more layers, because he intended to go outside. "Wait a minute. What're you going to do out there?"

"We need more firewood, whether I can find something to split it with or not. I put the last log I'd brought in on the fire about an hour ago."

"But your hair is still wet."

"Not for long." He scrubbed the towel roughly over his hair.

She went to the hall closet and unzipped the front pocket of the suitcase that sat inside on the floor and pulled out a cashmere scarf. The coordinating leather gloves would never fit him in a million years, nor would the secondhand coat she'd bought, but she took them out, anyway. If she went outside, she'd need them.

"I know," she said when he finally unearthed his head from the towel and saw the scarf she was holding. "*More* pink. But it'll help keep your head warm. I don't have a hat to my name, unfortunately."

"Beggars can't be choosers." He took the scarf and wrapped it awkwardly over his head.

She tsked. "Here. Let me." She reworked the cashmere smoothly over his tousled hair, twisted it, and wrapped it twice around his neck before tucking in the ends.

She accidentally caught his gaze with hers. His thick brown

eyelashes had dark gold tips, she realized. Basically the same burnished color as the faint beard blurring his sharp jaw. He also had a tiny scar that bisected the end of his left eyebrow.

She quickly stepped back, deliberately halting her visual feast. "Fashionable *and* functional."

"Thank God Devaney can't see me now," he muttered, and pulled on his bomber jacket, zipping it all the way to his throat.

"Who's Devaney?"

"A guy I work with."

"I wish I had gloves that would fit you. Would it help to wear socks over your hands?"

"Like mittens? Sure."

She found another pair. Her last, and this time they were purple with blue polka dots. She'd deliberately purchased the most colorful multipack she could find at the discount store because her mother would have detested them.

Childish, maybe. But infinitely satisfying.

She held them out. "Here you go."

He pushed his hands inside them. "I've even been accused a time or two of not having opposable thumbs, so socks are just about perfect. Wish me luck." He pulled open the door, stepped out and quickly shut it behind him.

She pulled aside the curtain again, to watch him head down the steps. When he reached the ground, he sank into the snow nearly to his knees. It didn't stop him, though, and she watched until he turned the corner of the house and moved out of sight.

She hurriedly gathered together a clean pair of jeans and a long-sleeved T-shirt and went into the bathroom, dragging them on. There was still enough warm water left to wash her face and clean her teeth, and she pulled a brush through her hair, taming it enough to toss it up in a clip. Then she pulled on the same thick sweater she'd worn the day before.

Her appearance-conscious mother would have been appalled.

She didn't care. Aside from her coat, the sweater was the warmest thing she owned. She laced her stocking feet into tennis shoes and immediately her chilly toes felt warmer.

She folded up the blankets, then manhandled the recalcitrant bed back into the couch, and replaced the cushions.

There was still hot water in the saucepan Darr had used, but not enough for much more than another cup of tea, which she didn't want anyway. To her, it just seemed that herbal tea was a poor substitute for fresh-ground coffee. So she added more water to the pot, dumped in a measure of quick-cooking oats and, feeling quite pioneerlike, carried the pan over to the fireplace, moved the screen and nudged the pot in next to the grate. The pan was entirely metal, so she doubted it would suffer any harm.

With a wooden spoon and a folded towel to use as a pot holder, she sat on the hearth and watched the pot, pulling it out occasionally to stir it.

Before long, the contents looked as if she'd cooked them right on the stove.

Feeling ridiculously pleased, she moved the pot to the hearth and plopped a cover on it. When Darr came in from the cold, at least she'd be able to offer him something warm for his stomach.

She replaced the fireplace screen and went to the window and peeked out again. He'd obviously made the trek to his truck because she could see the deep trench of footprints he'd left. Of him, however, there was still no sign. She went to the refrigerator. She didn't want to let out any more cold air than necessary, but she opened it quickly just to extract the plastic bowl of fruit she kept on the top shelf next to the milk.

Humming under her breath, she stood at the sink and

started peeling a large orange. The people on the cooking shows she occasionally caught on PBS made the task look much easier than it was. By the time Bethany was finished, the sections were more than a little mangled, and she was sticky with juice up to her wrists, just like usual. She dumped the pieces in a bowl and rinsed her hands, then started on a gigantic green apple. She made a better job of that, at least, courtesy of the sharp knife she'd bought at the grocery store.

She heard the rattle of the doorknob, and turned to see Darr enter with a few logs in his arms. He'd obviously made some attempt at brushing the caked snow from the legs of his jeans, but patches of it still clung to the denim and when he nudged the door behind him shut with the heel of his boot, a clump fell onto the carpet.

"No luck on the axe or a hatchet. Or anything else useful, for that matter." He carried the wood to the fireplace and started stacking it on the edge of the brick hearth. "The logs seemed to stay dry from the shelter of the carport, but they'll be slower to burn than if they were split."

"Won't that make the wood last longer?"

"Yup. Harder to get burning and slower to heat, too." He pulled the socks off his hands, then shrugged out of his jacket, eyeing the covered pot sitting on the hearth. "What's that?"

"Oatmeal." She hurried forward and using the folded towel, moved it out of his way. "Breakfast is the most important meal and all that."

"I'd have been happy with cold leftover spaghetti. Oatmeal is great." He unwound the pink scarf from his head. His thick hair stuck out in spikes and her fingers itched to smooth through it. "Anything warm sounds great. It's colder than a witch's tongue out there."

She couldn't seem to get the smile off her face and turned

back to the kitchen. "I cut up some fruit, too." She quickly set everything on the table. "Cook—" She realized what she was saying and bit off the rest of the thoughtless sentence. That Cook had always served oatmeal with raisins and brown sugar.

"What about cooking?" He pulled out one of the chairs at the table, obviously for her, and she slipped onto the seat.

"Oh." She shook her head. "Cooking isn't my forte, that's all. Not with a proper stove, much less over a wood fire. I, um, I hope the oatmeal isn't too lumpy."

He reached for the bowl of fruit and spooned some right on top of his cereal then tucked in. "It's fine." He let out a quick breath. "And hot."

She quickly hopped up again to fill a water glass. "Here."

"Thanks." He gulped down a third of the glass, then stuck his spoon right back into the hot cereal, giving every indication that he was perfectly satisfied with the ordinary fare. "So what do you want to do today, Barbara?"

"Do?" She eyed that scar on his eyebrow and wondered if he'd earned it on the job. "I don't know." She nibbled at an apple wedge.

"What would you ordinarily do on a Sunday if you weren't snowed in with a stranger?"

"Do laundry. Clean." Her lips quirked. "It takes hours to keep this place up, you know, being as palatial as it is."

His dimple flashed. "Anything else?"

"I don't know. Read. Take a nap. We pregnant women are big on naps."

"Ain't that the truth." He added more fruit to his bowl, leaving her to wonder if he knew that fact just in a general sense, or if it was from more personal experience.

From his tone, it had sounded personal and she quickly realized just how little she really knew about Darr.

He wore no rings, but what did that really matter? For all she knew, he had a girlfriend, five ex-wives and a half-dozen kids.

Just as rapidly, she dismissed the notion.

He wasn't the secretive one. She was.

"Laundry is out, obviously," he went on. "Cleaning'll take about three minutes, I'm figuring. Maybe five. Being so palatial and all." His gaze lifted, and settled on her face. "Better all around to leave napping to you."

"I suppose you're too macho to indulge in such behavior?"

The corner of his lips kicked up. He looked amused and very, *very* wry. "Too smart," he said.

Before she could decipher that, he tapped the edge of her bowl with his spoon. "Eat up. You'll want something hot in your stomach when we go out."

Bemusement slid through her. "We're going out?"

"Might as well. Better than twiddling our thumbs indoors when we don't have to. Do you know if anyone lives in the house down the hill?"

"As far as I know." She hadn't made a point of meeting whoever did, though. For one thing, she didn't know how long she'd be able to stay in Red Rock. For another, it was hard enough keeping up her false identity with her coworkers, much less even more people, like neighbors. "There's a car that comes and goes."

"Good enough for me. We'll check on them. See if they're okay. Maybe they'll have an axe we can borrow. Unless you'd rather not go with me?"

"No. That's fine." The truth was, it didn't really matter how they passed the time.

She couldn't think of anyone she'd rather be with even if they did absolutely nothing at all.

While she finished her oatmeal and fruit, he fiddled with

the logs in the fire. Whatever he did was effective enough to get a small flame started.

She imagined that after being outside for a while, it might actually be strong enough to create a small amount of heat.

Then he pulled on his jacket and the sock-mittens, and she pulled the used wool peacoat over her thick sweater and fitted her hands into the fine leather gloves. "Here." He tossed her the scarf.

"Don't you want it?"

"Head's not wet anymore. And the color suits you better."

"I don't know about that," she countered lightly. She was rapidly coming to the conclusion that Darr Fortune looked pretty darn fine in almost anything. But she slid the scarf around her neck and tucked the ends into her collar. The only thing she couldn't do anything about was her tennis shoes. She had nothing else she could wear. The shoes that she wore to the office would have been even more unsuitable.

"After you, ma'am." He opened the door and held out his arm.

She stepped out onto the porch. The air was clear and so crisp with cold that it stung a little just breathing it in. It was also silent. Sparkling. Amazingly beautiful.

"Come on." He took her hand. "Careful on the steps. I didn't notice ice earlier, but you never know."

When they reached the bottom, her tennis shoes promptly sank several inches into the snow and she couldn't help but laugh. "I feel like I have on cement galoshes." She lifted her hands to her sides. "Now what?"

"When's the last time you were around snow?"

"Last year on a skiing trip." She'd worn knee-high designer boots and a mink coat that Lyle had insisted on giving her, despite her distaste for real fur. As expert on the slopes as he was with everything else, he hadn't wanted to slow down enough to match her more elementary level. While he'd spent hours on the slopes, she'd spent hours alone in the lodge.

She should have recognized that something was lacking when she hadn't missed his company in the least.

"You ski?"

"Not very well."

He grinned. "Me, neither. I'm better on water skis, and even that ain't too pretty of a picture."

She strongly doubted that.

"Just follow in my footsteps. And if you get too tired, say so, and we'll stop."

"You make it sound like we're climbing the Himalayas." But she fell in step behind him. Not surprisingly, he was right about following in the path he cut before her. She suspected that he was dragging his boots more than he ordinarily would have to clear the way for her; regardless; it was effective. She didn't even have snow sliding down inside the tops of her shoes.

They stopped when they reached his truck, though. He used his arm to sweep away some of the snow and he tried to open the door, but couldn't.

"Did you lock it?"

"Nope. It's frozen." He squinted up at the gray sky. "Come on. You still doing okay?"

A bubble of laughter rose in her throat. "I'm pregnant, not decrepit. We haven't even made it halfway to the road, yet. And I'm fine."

"Okay." He took her at her word and headed past the truck. "Watch that rut," he pointed behind him. "Your drive needs some serious grading."

"Tell me something I don't know. I got the owners to knock some off the rent because of it." She'd been quite proud of herself for negotiating that little matter in her favor.

"I suppose that means they don't intend to fix it anytime soon."

"I'll take the discounted rent over the grading."

He made a sound, not much more than a grunt, that she didn't bother deciphering.

Everyone had their priorities. Living as frugally as she could now meant that her savings would last just that much longer when she had to take time off for the baby.

Or if she had to bolt, again.

She was strongly hoping that wouldn't be the case, though. Everything about Red Rock and her life there was the antithesis of the life she'd led before. But she *liked* the town far more than she'd anticipated when she'd deliberately chosen to settle there. The people were friendly without being too nosy. The town itself was as picturesque as a postcard. Even her small rented house had its charms.

Her foot slipped on the snow but she caught herself before falling.

That's what she got for keeping her eyes glued to the charms of the rear view in front of her, and not where she was walking.

When they made it to the road, she was glad to find that the snow didn't seem as deep. She still followed in Darr's wake, though, and by the time they made it to the bottom of the hill where the closest house was located, her muscles were feeling loose and warm despite the cold temperature that had turned her nose into an ice cube.

Darr bounded up the three steps to the front door and knocked loudly. "Anyone home?"

After his second round of knocking, the door squeaked open and a baleful eye glared out at them. "What do you want?"

"We're from up the road," Darr said easily. "Just wanted to check and see that everyone here is all right."

"And what wouldcha do if I wasn't?" the man barked.

"See if I could help, sir. I'm Lieutenant Fortune with the Red Rock Fire Department."

The door cracked open a little farther. Enough to reveal a shock of wiry white hair and a wrinkled face that looked just as cantankerous as the voice sounded. "My tax dollars paying for the fire department to go door to door? Like a man don't have enough to pay for without that?"

"Actually, I'm not on duty. But we would go door to door if we had to. Is your electricity out?"

"Ain't it out all over town?" He looked over at Bethany where she was waiting at the foot of the steps. "We got lady firemen now, I suppose." His tone made it plain what he thought of *that*.

"Yes, we do," Darr agreed. "But—"

"But I'm not one of them," Bethany inserted. "I live up there." She pointed toward the hill behind them. Now that they were standing still, even for just a few minutes, she could feel the cold seeping through her jeans.

"Fenton's place." The man squinted at her, obviously judging. "You're the blonde who drives that blue beater with the bad brakes. Better get 'em fixed, girlie, or one day you'll drive down off this road and keep on going."

She felt herself flush.

"We'll get that taken care of," Darr told the man. "Are you able to keep warm enough? Have enough food? Water?"

The man looked irritated that Darr would even ask. "Hell, boy, I got me a generator. You young kids. Never think to be prepared. That's the problem with the world today."

Darr grinned and Bethany realized that the more ornery the old man sounded, the more cheerful Darr seemed to get. "You're probably right about that," he said. "So maybe you can bail *us* out. You wouldn't happen to have an axe or a hatchet we could borrow?"

The man heaved a grunting sigh. "Hold on." He slammed the door shut.

"Friendly," Bethany murmured under her breath.

Darr chuckled. "Reminds me of the captain I had when I was a probie. Guy was grouchy as hell but he had a heart of gold." Footsteps crunching on the snow interrupted, and they looked over to the side of the house to see the old man, now bundled in a hooded parka with his khaki-colored pants pushed untidily into the tops of fur-lined boots. "Here." He shoved a long-handled axe at Darr. "Better get your butts back up the hill," he advised, glaring at them both. "Snow's going to start falling again soon. I can smell it."

"Well, you're a lot more prepared for it than most folks around here," Darr told him. He held the axe just below the head. "I'll get this back to you as soon as I can."

"Eh." The old man waved his hand. "I got others." His faded blue eyes squinted at Bethany. "She can drop it off sometime when she's squeaking her way past my house."

"Appreciate that." Darr pulled the sock off his hand and stuck it out.

The man grimaced, but pulled off his own thick glove to shake Darr's hand. "John Decker," he provided grudgingly. Then he pulled off the other glove. "Here. You can bring them back, too, when you're done. Don't argue," he barked, when Darr paused. "Can't abide arguing fools."

"Yes, sir." Darr took the gloves. "Thank you, again."

"Yes. Thank you, Mr. Decker," Bethany added.

The man gave that same annoyed grunt. He stomped up his steps and pushed through his front door. It closed unceremoniously behind him.

Darr exchanged the socks for the gloves, then balled up the socks and pushed them into his pockets. "Back up the hill we go. You still doing okay?"

"I'm fine." She strode past him, reversing the way along the path they'd already made. "Just because I'm pregnant doesn't mean I'm out of shape," she said over her shoulder. "I used to run marathons, for heaven's sake."

"Yeah? Which ones?"

"Los Angeles. Chicago. New York. I was drawn in the lottery for that one two years ago."

"Houston?"

"Oh, yeah. Every year." She snapped her mouth shut.

"I run to train, but never got involved in the marathon thing. When'd you start?"

"In high school." It was the only thing at which she'd managed to excel. Her mother had hated it, deeming it unladylike. Her father had pretty much patted her on the head, calling it just one more of her silly phases. "You?" The road started to climb.

"About then. Do you run now?"

"Not since I moved here—oh!" The sole of her tennis shoe slid on the gravel and she started to pitch forward, but Darr's arm slid around her from behind, scooping her back against him.

"Steady there." His breath was warm against her ear.

Even through all the layers she wore, she was excruciatingly aware of the press of his thickly gloved hand under her breasts; of the solid wall of him behind her. "Thanks." Her voice shook and there didn't seem to be one thing she could do to change it. Not when both her pulse and her hormones seemed to be skittering around as if in a hot pan. "You, um, you always seem to be rescuing me."

His arm around her seemed to tighten fractionally. "I can think of worse things."

Her heart was climbing toward her throat. Her gloved hands slid over his, but she didn't know if that was to push his hold away or to keep him from pulling away. "Darr—"

His head lowered. His jaw grazed her temple. "Just answer a question for me."

She turned her head, looking up at him, and felt everything inside her grind to a breathless halt. "What?"

"The night of the fire, you said there was no one for us to call for you. No husband. No boyfriend. Was that the truth?"

"Yes." That at least was the bald, naked truth.

"Good," he muttered, and pressed his mouth to hers.

Chapter Five

Darr felt her quick intake of breath; the momentary shock that stiffened her. And almost as quickly, everything about her softened. Most particularly her lips.

He'd kissed plenty of women in his life. But nothing, *no one,* was like kissing Barbara.

She murmured something against his mouth, but he didn't hear. All he knew was that her gloved hand was sliding around his neck, that she was turning toward him, that her mouth was the warmest, sweetest thing he'd ever tasted.

When she finally pulled away, gasping, pressing her forehead against his shoulder, it took all of his willpower not to lift her face to his and kiss her again. He closed his eyes, tilting his head back, and pictured Devaney's ugly mug. Anything to cool the fire raging inside him.

His leather jacket creaked when she lifted her head again, trailed her gloved hands down his chest. "It's snowing again." Her voice was faint. Her indigo eyes looked dazed.

The blood that should have kept his brain functioning had all headed south and he stared stupidly up at the fat white flakes dancing down from the solidly gray sky. She shifted, pulling away from him and he reluctantly released her. Realized he'd dropped the axe in the snow beside them.

She stepped beyond the path he'd made down the hill and lifted her arms out from her sides, looking upward. A soft laugh bubbled out of her. "Again. It's snowing *again*. Can you believe it?" She looked back at him. "What are the odds?"

What were the odds of falling in love with a woman practically at first sight?

"Astronomical," he murmured.

"I'll say." The smile playing around her lips suddenly turned impish. It was the only warning he had before she leaned over, packed up a handful of snow, and tossed it at him.

The snowball exploded softly when it hit him square in the shoulder.

"Oh. Honey." He clucked his tongue. "What was that for?"

She grinned. "Isn't that what we're supposed to do in the snow?"

He slowly, deliberately leaned over and scooped John Decker's sturdy, lined glove through the snow. Straightened and just as slowly, just as deliberately, packed the other glove around it.

Her eyes were laughing. "You're not going to throw that at me. You're the heroic type, remember? An all-around nice guy?"

"Nah." He tossed the solid ball from one hand to the other. "When it comes to water fights and snowballs—" he caught the ball in his right hand and narrowed his eyes "—I fight back."

Her hair flew out over her shoulders when she turned on

her heel, doing her best to jog through the snow, though it kept swallowing her legs nearly to her knees. She forged on, though, high-stepping diagonally away from the road toward her house. He pitched the snowball and it splattered square and harmless between her shoulder blades.

She turned, laughing, and grabbed up another mound of snow, gained several feet up the hill, then turned again and launched it at him, this time catching him right in the chest.

She pumped her arm triumphantly and darted away again, only to stop short, laughing even harder. "Wait, wait," she called as he closed the distance between them, another snowball already forming in his hands. "Time out!"

"Tired of the game already?"

She giggled and raised her foot, wriggling her stocking toes. "I lost my shoe in the snow."

"Excuses, excuses." He lobbed the snowball at her and it hit her dead center in the chest. She screeched, and started to fall, arms cartwheeling for balance.

But it was no good.

Cursing at himself, he plowed across the distance, but there was no way to reach her before she fell backward. "Barbara!" He slid the last foot on his knees and tore off his gloves, tossing them aside.

He slid his bare hand along her neck. She was trembling, her gloved hand pressed to her mouth. "Don't move. I'm sorry. I don't know what the hell I was thinking. Where do you hurt?"

"I'm not hurt!" She dropped her hand, and he realized she was laughing. "I have a foot of snow underneath me, remember?"

His relief was swift and all-encompassing. "I still shouldn't have thrown that snowball at you."

"There are worse things." Her voice was a little too blithe; a little too deliberate. "Nice aim, by the way." She grinned up at him, and that at least seemed completely genuine. "I have snow down my coat."

"We should get you inside."

"Wait." She tilted her head back in the mattress of snow. "Snow angels first." Suiting words to action, she slowly worked her arms up and down, her legs in and out. Her long hair was splayed around her head and a few snowflakes settled among the curls. "Come on," she chided. "Don't you like snow angels?"

The snow angel he was looking at was pretty damn appealing. "I'll leave that to you," he said gruffly, "and look for your shoe."

Her swishing limbs stopped. She pushed up on her elbows and dashed a snowflake off her eyelash. Her humor had just as effectively been dashed judging by the suddenly stubborn set of her chin. "I'm not that incompetent. I can find my own shoe. Where's the axe?"

"Nobody said anything about incompetence." He pulled on the borrowed gloves again, pushed to his feet and headed back to where he'd dropped the axe. The heavy head was buried in the snow; the long handle sticking up like a periscope. He pulled it out of the snow and turned back toward Barbara.

Over the snowy hillside, their footprints were like a crisscrossing map. She was hop-stepping her way around, obviously trying to keep her shoeless foot out of the snow as she searched for her tennis shoe. He could tell the instant she found it, for she immediately sat down on her rear and pulled it on.

Around them, the snow was falling a little faster. A little harder. He reached her and held out his hand to her.

She put her hand in his and he pulled her to her feet. "I'm sorry I snapped at you," she murmured.

He shrugged. "You said what you thought."

She dashed the snow from the seat of her pants with a swish of her hands. "I…well, I guess I'm used to people thinking I'm incompetent."

He couldn't help wondering *what* people. But she didn't offer more of an explanation, and he didn't ask. "Come on. We'd better get back to the house. I want to get some wood split while I can."

She sucked in her lip for half a second, then turned and dug her shoes into the snow, heading upward. By the time they made it to the porch, their original footprints were starting to fill in with fresh snowfall and the fog of their breath was even more visible. "I'll heat up something over the fire for us to drink," she said before going inside.

He continued around to the stack of wood tucked under the carport.

He'd worked his way through a decent stack of logs and into a sweat when he felt the buzzing of his cell phone against his chest. He notched the blade into the upstanding log he was using as a base and pulled out the phone. Nick. "Yeah. Who's sick?"

"Nobody. It's not like with Mom," his brother said speedily.

Darr leaned his weight against the end of axe handle and let out a long breath. "Thank God," he murmured. "Then what'd Patrick want to talk about so badly?"

"It's complicated." Nick's voice was muffled, as if he didn't particularly want to be overheard. "You still stuck out there with Blondie?"

"Barbara. And yeah."

"Hmm. Cozy."

Darr pinched his eyes shut. He didn't want to think about how cozy. And judging by the continuing snowfall, they had another night under the same roof ahead of them.

For one night, she'd been glad of his presence. What would happen after another night?

More to the point, what would happen *now,* when he'd put the monumentally ill-advised moves on her? She hadn't exactly beat him off with a stick.

But she was pregnant, and wariness screamed off her like a neon light.

"Earth to Darwin," Nick's voice slowly penetrated. "Yo, bro. You still there or not?"

He focused. "I'm here. The power out at the ranch, too?"

"Yeah, but Lily's well equipped with generators. Nobody is suffering too badly. You?"

The only suffering Darr was undergoing was owed entirely to jonesing for a woman he should know well enough to stay away from. "She's got at least half a cord of wood and I borrowed an axe from a neighbor. We're doing all right. You going to tell me what's *complicated,* or do I have to guess?"

"You could try, but believe me. You wouldn't guess. Hold on. I'm going outside for a sec." Darr could hear muffled murmuring, then Nick came back on the line. "Too many freaking people here," his brother muttered in a clearer voice. "God, I cannot believe it is snowing again. Sometime, remind me why I let you convince me that moving here was a good thing."

Darr let that one pass. The truth was, if Nick hadn't been ready to leave California, he wouldn't have left, no matter what anyone said.

He worked the axe loose and dropped the blade again into the base log. "So, what's the deal?"

Nick heaved a sigh. "Evidently, someone slipped a note into Patrick's pocket at the New Year's Eve party Emmett and Linda threw." Emmett Jamison and his wife ran the

Fortune Foundation, and they'd rented out Red for the private party. "At least Patrick figures it was during the party. He didn't even notice it until a few days later. Basically says something to the effect that one of the Fortunes is not who we think."

"What the hell is that supposed to mean?" Darr recalled the lively party and those present. The Fortune family was admittedly extensive, and they'd been well-represented at the party. So, too, had been a lot of the Mendozas. Not only did José and Maria Mendoza own the restaurant, but the Fortune and Mendoza families had long been friends.

"Good question. Patrick might have shrugged it off as a joke, except that Dad received a similar one."

"What?"

"And get this. Aunt Cindy got one, too."

"Hell." There was no pretending that was coincidence. Cindy's life had been too far removed from the rest of the Fortunes. "Was there a demand for money or something?"

"No. Not yet. That's where they think this might be heading, of course. Cindy wants to call in Ross to get to the bottom of it."

Darr squinted. Overhead, the carport creaked. Ross, a private detective, was Cindy's eldest. "I thought he and Cindy didn't speak these days."

"As far as I know, they don't. But he's just over in San Antonio and she figures he's not likely to turn down a good-paying job. He can nose around without being entirely noticeable. Everyone seemed to agree that it was a good idea."

"If he agrees." There was no love lost between Ross and his mother.

"There's that."

Standing inactive was accomplishing nothing but making

him cold, and Darr leaned over, grabbing up another log. "I'm surprised Dad didn't say something to us earlier."

"Until Patrick and he both realized they'd gotten similar notes, I don't think either one paid much attention. It's not like the Fortunes haven't been targets of all sorts of nonsense over the years. Anyway, that's the deal here."

"Yeah, well, at least nobody's dying." That's the only thing he cared about. As for anonymous notes and the motives behind them, he couldn't begin to venture a guess. Darr yanked the axe loose again and balanced the log on its rough-hewn end. "Call me if anything else comes up."

"Will do."

He shut off the phone and stuck it back inside his jacket, then swung the axe down onto the end of the log. It split clean in two. He quartered the halves, left the axe buried in the base, and began carrying the rest inside.

Barbara was sitting on the narrow brick hearth, a folded dish towel in her hand. When he entered, she turned toward the door, a smile on her face. "I made hot chocolate. Over the fire."

He pushed his heart back down out of his throat. You'd think he'd never seen a beautiful woman before. "Sounds good." He nudged the door shut behind him and carried the wood to the fireplace, crouching down to stack it against the wall.

"If you'd rather have coffee, I could make that instead. Fortunately, my coffee grinder runs on batteries."

He'd seen the grinder on the shelf. A fancy little device. And her coffee beans were top of the line, too, he knew.

Then he reminded himself that how she spent her money was no business of his.

"Hot chocolate is fine." In fact, the aroma was filling the cottage, right along with the warmth from the fireplace. Warmth that she must be feeling, too, since she'd peeled off her socks as well as that oversize sweater, leaving a pink long-sleeved shirt behind that clung to the high, full thrust of her breasts. "Let me get the rest of the wood I split, though, first."

She nodded, leaning forward to move the handle of the pot she was using for the hot chocolate. The V of her neckline gaped, giving him a gut-tightening glimpse of creamy flesh cupped by snug white lace.

He dragged his gaze away and bolted for the door, then nearly fell on his butt when his boot slid on one of the steps outside. He caught the iron rail, and shoved his glove through his hair, letting the cold air flow over him.

Maybe if he rolled around in the snow for a while, his jets would cool, too.

He stomped around the side of the house again and pushed several handfuls of kindling into his pockets before grabbing up the rest of the wood he'd cut. The wind was steadily picking up. He couldn't tell how much was fresh snow coming down and how much was just being blown around. Snow had even drifted up beneath the outer corners of the carport, banking against the tires of Barbara's car.

They'd have to shovel some out before she'd be able to move her car. Clearly, there was no point in making a start on that task just yet.

Arms loaded, he retraced his steps back to the front door. Barbara must have been watching for him because she opened the door before he could maneuver a hand free for the knob.

"Let me help you," she said, grabbing several pieces off the top before he could protest. She added them to the stack beside the fireplace then quickly moved out of the way for him to do the same. "It looks like we could heat this place for the next week with all this wood."

"You're fortunate there was a healthy supply here." He

emptied his pockets of the wood chips and long slivers, leaving the kindling more or less neatly in a pile to the other side of the hearth, and then peeled out of his jacket. The multiple layers of T-shirts followed. When he'd pulled them all off, he yanked his department blues back over his head and leaned down to start on his boots and the socks.

Barbara set a mug on the coffee table, complete with a folded napkin and a heart-shaped red-and-white lollipop, before settling in the side chair.

"Someone was giving those out at the Foundation office," she said when he picked it up and twirled the stick between his fingers. "For Valentine's Day. It's peppermint."

"That's right. I'd forgotten today was the 14th." He lifted the lollipop in a toast. "Happy Valentine's Day."

"You, too." She held an identical candy in her hand and swirled the heart through her own mug, then popped it between her soft lips. After a moment, she slid it back out and dunked it in her mug again. "Not bad."

He realized he was staring at the slick gleam left behind on her pink lips and yanked the wrapper off his own candy, shoving it in his mouth. "Isn't there caffeine in hot chocolate?" he asked around it.

"A little. Not anything like coffee. My doctor suggested it. She also said I could stand the extra calories." She made a face and pulled her shirt taut against her belly. "Like I'm not getting big enough as it is."

He exhaled carefully and moved away, carrying his various shirts over to one of the table chairs. To buy himself time to get some control over the need raging through him, he made a production of draping them over the back of it for the next time he needed to wear them.

The wind whistled around the cottage, hitting the windowpane in soft beats. The fire crackled. He flipped on the light switch next to the refrigerator, but there was still no power.

The candy was spicy against his tongue, but it still wasn't strong enough to remove the taste of the kiss they'd shared.

He crunched it into pieces and tossed the stick into the small trash can tucked beneath her sink, then looked back at her. She was staring into the fire, sliding the lollipop around inside her mouth.

God. He was dying.

"What games?" he asked abruptly.

She jumped a little and her blue gaze slanted his way. She drew out the candy and pressed her lips together for a moment. "Excuse me?"

"Earlier, you said the owners left some board games."

Her forehead smoothed. "Right." She pushed off the chair, dropped the lollipop in the trash and went to the closet that opened off the short hallway. She rummaged around for a minute. Pulled out a very expensive piece of rolling luggage. "Sorry. It's a little cramped in here." She rummaged around a little more. Out came a few flat, colorful boxes, and the suitcase was rolled back inside out of sight. She picked up the game boxes and moved them to the coffee table. "Take your pick."

Chutes and Ladders. Twister. Monopoly.

"Monopoly," he said wryly.

"I figured." She smiled faintly and ran her hand over her abdomen as she sat on the side chair again. "With this one, the only thing in my future is going to be Chutes and Ladders. And I think Twister is definitely a thing of the past for me."

He couldn't recall the last time he'd played the human-pretzel game, but his imagination had no trouble conjuring up images of the two of them playing. Whether she was five months' pregnant or not.

He grimly pulled the top off the Monopoly box. He needed to get those sorts of thoughts out of his brain or he'd be a raving lunatic before too long. "You want to be banker or should I?" She didn't answer and he looked at her. She was nibbling the inside of her lip, her hands folded neatly in her lap. "Something wrong?"

Her fingers lifted slightly. "You tell me. You're the one who seems…upset."

"Just cabin fever," he dismissed. A convenient excuse and much better than admitting that he was aching for her right to his back teeth. He unfolded the game board on the coffee table. It was such a well-used game that the cardboard nearly split apart at the seams. "Pick your piece." He dumped the playing pieces on the corner of the board closest to her.

She didn't look exactly convinced but she reached out and selected the car.

"I'd have pegged you for the Scotty dog piece," he drawled. He'd keep it light, or die trying.

"You just wanted the car for yourself," she returned and set her piece on *Go.* "Like all typical men."

He took the dog for himself and dumped the rest of the unused pieces back into the box. "Played plenty of Monopoly then, have you?"

"A time or two. When we were younger." She slid out of the chair to sit on the floor beside the table.

"Your brother liked the car," he deduced.

She picked up the stack of property cards. "And my father liked the money," she murmured. "You can do the banking. I'll do the title deeds. Unless you're one of those stick-to-the-rules kind of guys where the banker handles it all." She squared the cards with a tap on the table, waiting.

"There are a few rules I live by—" namely not taking advantage of vulnerable women "—but that's not one of them."

She began organizing the cards on the floor beside her. "What are they? The rules."

"We each get $1,500.00 to start."

She looked at him from beneath her lashes. "*Your* rules. Not the game."

He rifled through the play money. "Don't lie."

She glanced back at the cards she was laying out. He strongly wished that it was just coincidence, but the prickling at the back of his neck warned him otherwise. "Don't cheat," he added as if he hadn't noticed a single thing. "And don't steal."

"That's all?"

"They tend to cover most everything, literally or otherwise."

She laid out the last deed card and leaned her elbow on the coffee table. "I suppose they do, at that." She toyed with the dice that were lying on the board. "So are we playing for a set time or until you go bankrupt?"

Despite the prickling at his nape and her obvious change of subject, he grinned. "You didn't learn much by that snowball exchange, did you?"

"Just pass me my money and roll the dice. And then we'll see."

What they would see, he decided sometime later, was that whoever had taught her to play the game had taught her well. Fortunately for him, though economics hadn't been his career path, whiling away hours between emergency calls usually entailed some sort of pastime and he was no slouch at the game, either.

They were pretty much dead even as they broke to have some lunch—cold tuna sandwiches and canned tomato soup that she heated over the fire—and had begun playing second pieces just to spice it up when the gray light angled from afternoon toward evening and snow still spit from the sky. They'd pushed the coffee table out of the way, moved the game to the floor, and had even resorted to creating more money to supplement the bank's depleted supply.

"You're a cutthroat," he announced, not for the first time, when he landed on one of her building-laden properties to the tune of wiping out a substantial portion of his personal bank account.

"Maybe with the game," she demurred, taking the hefty rent he forfeited to her and adding it to her neat, orderly piles. By contrast, his cash was spread haphazardly next to him. His dwindling cash, that was.

"In real life?"

She shook her head. "Not so much or I wouldn't be here." She rolled the dice, and made a face when she landed on one of his particularly well-endowed properties. She handed back some of the money she'd just taken from him. "That's the fourth time I've landed on Park Place!"

She may have snatched up more properties, but he'd snagged his share, including the two biggies—Park Place and Boardwalk. With hotels, the resulting "rent" was nothing to sneeze at. "And my wallet appreciates it." He dropped the money on his pile. He knew if they called it quits, she'd be the winner with more assets, but he didn't really care. Continuing the game was as good a way to pass the time as any other.

Well. It was a safer way, at least.

"If you weren't here, where else would you be?" he asked.

Only the width of the tattered playing board separated them. "Nowhere interesting," she said, and leaned back against the pillow that she'd propped under her side. She stretched her arms over her head and pointed her toes—back inside socks once more—toward the fire. "Oh." Her hand went back to her abdomen.

"Are you all right?"

"Yes. The baby's moving." She shot him a bemused look. "I'm still not used to it."

"Do you know if it's a boy or a girl?"

"Not yet." Her lashes were lowered in concentration as her hand slowly drifted along her abdomen. "I have an ultrasound scheduled next week. If I want to find out then, they'll probably be able to tell me."

The motion of her hand was doing a good job of pulling the soft fabric of her shirt snug against her breasts.

He tried not to notice.

But he was a guy.

He noticed.

He absently rolled the dice and didn't even complain when he landed on the Go to Jail square. "Do you want to know?"

"I haven't decided yet," she mused thoughtfully. "On one hand, I'd like to wait and learn when the baby is born. On the other hand, knowing now would make it easier when I hit the secondhand store to find baby clothes." Her smile turned wry. "Not that an infant cares *what* color he or she is wearing. I just prefer blue or pink over that ever-neutral yellow. Green isn't my particular favorite, either. Fortunately, at the shop I found in San Antonio there doesn't seem to be a shortage of baby gear in any color. I'll sell you my Get Out of Jail card for a hundred dollars."

"Shark." The usual fee was only fifty. "I'll pass. What about a crib? Where will you put that?"

"I haven't figured that out yet. I wasn't even sure I'd be here when the baby came." She rolled onto her side, propped up on her elbow and reached for the dice.

"Got a bigger place in mind?"

"I meant *here* as in Red Rock."

"Town is a good place for kids." He kept his voice reasonable, though his neck was prickling like crazy. "The Foundation offers child care for its employees. Why would you want to leave that?"

"I wouldn't." She rolled the dice. "Not unless I had to."

"Why would you have to?"

She exhaled softly. "Darr—"

"Look, Barbara." He abruptly took the direct route. "Why don't you just tell me what kind of trouble you're in? Maybe I can help."

An expressionless mask that didn't fool him for a second slid over her face. "There's no trouble."

"Okay, then whatever you're running from," he said evenly. "Is it the baby's father?" It was an obvious guess.

She pushed to her knees and then to her feet, scattering her stacks of Monopoly money. "I realize it goes against your very nature, but you don't have to rescue me from anything else, Darr." She stepped over the game board and around his feet and went to the kitchen area. "I imagine you're hungry. I, um, I'm not sure what to fix for supper. Unless it's more canned soup and sandwiches." She picked up the loaf of bread they'd left on the counter after lunch. "Not imaginative, I know, but at least I can manage to boil something over the fire without ruining it."

He pushed to his feet, too, and followed her. Tension screamed from her slender shoulders and he settled his fingers on one pink-clad shoulder. "Barbara—"

She winced. Her fingers squeezed the plastic-wrapped bread. "I don't cheat," she said abruptly. "And I don't steal. And I never used to lie."

He pulled the bread out of her hand before she finished squashing it to death. "I want to help," he said softly, "but I need to know what we're dealing with."

"Why?" Her lashes lifted. Confusion clouded her eyes. "Why does it even matter to you? I'm nobody!"

"No one is nobody," he countered. "Certainly not you. Not to me. And if I haven't managed to convey that after all these hours you've been stuck with me, then I guess I'm not as good at communicating as I thought."

"I don't want you feeling sorry for me."

"Believe me, that isn't one of the feelings that is plaguing me." If anything, he was feeling pretty sorry for himself, and pretty annoyed by that very fact. "Just tell me whatever it is and we'll go from there."

"Maybe I'm a bank robber on the run."

He snorted. "Right. Living low on the hog so as not to draw attention to yourself."

"Well," she made a face, "what if I told you it was some legal problem. What would you do? Help me hide out? Turn me in?"

"I'd do what I could to help you. But I don't believe it's something like that. The Foundation runs background checks on all of its employees. You obviously passed that."

"Barbara Burton passed that," she said wearily.

He tipped up her chin. "And who is she?" he asked quietly.

Her lips pressed together. A swallow worked down her throat. She looked braced for a blow. "A friend from school."

He let out a long breath and slid his arms around her, tucking her head beneath his chin.

Amazingly, she didn't try to pull away.

Finally, they were getting somewhere.

He listened to the snap of the wind outside the cottage. "And that would mean you are… who?"

Chapter Six

"Bethany," she whispered so easily she cringed. Where was the backbone she was supposed to have grown in the past two months? Gone in a blink simply because it felt so good, so safe, surrounded by Darr's arms? It didn't even seem to matter that she knew she couldn't trust her own judgment when it came to men. The truth just pushed at her lips until the words were out. "My name is Bethany. Bethany Burdett."

"Bethany," he repeated softly. "That feels like a much better fit than Barbara." He tucked his finger beneath her chin and nudged upward. "Bethany," he said again. "Why the pretense?"

"I didn't do anything illegal," she said swiftly. Except lie about who she was to everyone she'd encountered since escaping Dallas. "And using Barb's name wasn't to defraud anyone or anything." Her old friend was living in Paris, studying art and blissfully unaware of the mess in which Bethany had found herself.

"Good to know."

She frowned warily. "You believe me?"

"I think I can tell when you're lying."

"Great." She pulled out of his arms and reached for the loaf of bread again. There was only half a loaf left as it was, and she'd managed to squash half of *that*. "So you know I've been a liar all along." She could only imagine what he must think of her.

He caught her elbows and turned her inexorably to face him again. "What I *knew* is that there were a few things that didn't add up for me. What I suspected was that you're scared of something. Or someone. And now, knowing that you're not even using your own name, I'm more convinced of it than ever."

"All right. I'm a poor liar. And you've got hero-juice flowing in your veins instead of blood. But this isn't a fire. You don't have to pull me to safety. I…I have to do this myself."

"And when does the lie stop, Bethany? You're halfway to term. Do you want to bring your baby into a world where you're still running? Still pretending to be someone that you're not?"

"The only thing that is a pretense is my name," she countered swiftly. "Everything else about my life here is real. The most *real* it's ever been!"

"Why? Because you're shopping at secondhand stores instead of designer shops?"

She could feel the blood draining out of her head and swallowed back a wave of dizzying nausea. "I don't know what you mean."

He snorted. "You buy one of the most expensive brands of coffee beans that you won't let yourself drink. The cost of that suitcase in the closet alone would probably pay the rent on this place for half a year. You might be living frugally now,

Bethany, but I'd bet my salary that it's not something you're accustomed to."

"Spoiled rich girl just doesn't wash off the way you'd think."

His lips tightened, but his eyes never lost that calm, gentle quality.

Maybe that's why it was so dangerously easy to let herself trust him.

Darr never got that look in his eyes that Lyle had when he was irritated.

"I don't think you're spoiled. I think you're—" He broke off. Tilted his head back and closed his eyes for a moment. "God," he murmured. He looked back at her, evidently shaking off whatever he'd been about to say. "It's the baby's father. That's who you're hiding from, right?"

Her throat tightened. She nodded. It was the truth. Just not all of the truth. Her parents were as thorny a problem as the man she'd nearly married.

He pulled the bread out of her grasp yet again. Folded her cold hands inside his. "What happened?"

"It doesn't matter. It's over."

"It does matter, when you feel you have to hide who you are. Honey, that's your basic damn right as a human being!"

Her eyes stung. Why couldn't she have met a man like Darr instead of a man like Lyle?

She stared at Darr's hands wrapped around hers. Strength was in the wide, square palms, the long, blunt-tipped fingers.

Strength.

Not violence.

"The first time he hit me, he blamed it on too many cocktails at a charity benefit we'd just attended." Her voice was thin with the humiliation that still burned.

Darr's fingers twitched around her hands, but he said

nothing. Just waited. As if they had all the time in the world in that snowbound cottage for her to run down the countless mistakes she'd made.

"We'd been engaged for three months by then," she added. "Marrying him satisfied everyone. His family. My family." Particularly her family, but she hadn't realized just *how* much until the day of the wedding and in a fit of temper over her wanting to wear her pearls instead of the diamond choker he'd given her as a wedding gift, Lyle had coldly informed her about the financial arrangement between him and her father.

Darr slowly ran his thumb over the back of her knuckles. "And you? Did the idea of marrying him satisfy you?"

She frowned slightly. "It…I couldn't think of a reason to refuse. The only thing I was raised to do was land a husband like him. Successful. Wealthy."

"Did you love him?" His voice was even lower. Deeper.

"I'd known him since I was twenty-one. I thought I did." Even that admission burned. "Or maybe I just convinced myself that I did because everyone expected me to." She made a face. "It's a poor excuse, but if you knew me, you'd see…well. Anyway, I found out I was pregnant and suddenly there was something more important to focus on than finding exactly the right shade of dye for my bridesmaids' shoes, and deciding between Bavarian cream or lemon-curd filling for the wedding cake." Her throat tightened. "My…fiancé didn't embrace the idea when I told him about the baby." In fact, he'd been livid. He wanted a beautiful Texas debutante on his arm. Not a pregnant heifer.

"He's an ass," Darr said. "A real piece of sh—scum."

Since Bethany had come to that conclusion herself, she didn't see any reason to argue.

"You said the *first* time. He hit you again?"

The first time, she'd retreated to her parents, expecting them to be as fully horrified as she'd been. Her father had snapped at her to stop exaggerating a lover's tiff. Her mother had wailed that Bethany needed to beg, if she had to, to get back into Lyle's good graces before he called off the wedding. The second time, she'd showed them the bruises on her shoulders caused by Lyle's punishing hands, and they *still* accused her of some imagined hysteria caused by the elaborate wedding plans and rapidly approaching nuptials. The third time, she hadn't gone to her parents. Instead, she'd run out on all of them on the very day of her wedding.

Run out on her life.

And now, it was just her and her baby. And though she worried about the future, about being a good mother, about how she would make ends meet when the only thing she'd ever been trained to do was decorate the arm of a wealthy man, she didn't regret her actions for a second.

Except that she hadn't left for good after the first time.

"Sometimes I'm a slow learner," she said. About Lyle. About her parents.

Definitely about herself.

She drew in a shaking breath and let it out in a heady stream. "He's out of our life and I want to keep it that way."

"But you think he's looking for you. That's the reason for the assumed name."

She was certain of it. Lyle wouldn't stand for the public humiliation of his bride running out on him. The fact that he'd managed to keep it out of the news was simply a testament to the power he wielded as an up-and-coming power broker. The fact that his intended was the youngest daughter of one of the oldest, supposedly most oil-moneyed families in the entire state would only make the scandal that much more juicy.

"I don't want to take the chance, just in case he is," Bethany said carefully.

"You should have pressed charges against him."

Her father was drinking buddies with the sheriff and both of them were firmly in the good-ol'-boy mold. "Maybe. But leaving was my top priority."

He was watching her with hooded eyes. "That was a good move, too."

She knew it, but having Darr commend her for it was still unexpected. And unaccountably touching.

Inside her, the baby fluttered.

Awareness accosted her over just how closely the two of them were standing.

Of the way his thumb continued to stroke, warm and distracting, over her knuckles. The back of her hand. Again and again.

And just how alone they were there in her small, rented house. She and this man whose kiss had been intoxicatingly tempting.

She swallowed against her oddly parched throat. Moistened her dry lips. She knew the wisest course would be to move away from him. To make her trembling legs put some well-needed physical distance between the overwhelming appeal of him and her more-than-apparent vulnerability to it.

But next to *him* is right where she stayed. "Darr—"

"Is it going to freak you out if I kiss you again?"

She sucked in a quick breath.

His gaze burned over her face, dropped to her lips, then returned to her eyes. She felt warm from the inside out. "You didn't freak me out the first time," she reminded. The admission felt husky. Raw. "That probably says more about me than anything." She was a runaway bride, with an attraction to her snowed-in roommate that was escalating exponentially.

But there was no judgment in his blue eyes. Nothing but

warmth. And an odd glint of humor when his lips suddenly kicked up at the corner. "I don't know that it says anything at all. So I'll be the one to admit being a little freaked."

She felt a hot flush rise up her throat and start to crawl up her face. "If you didn't want to kiss me, then why did you?"

"I didn't say I didn't want to." He caught her face in his hands. "What's unsettling is how damn badly I didn't want to stop."

Then why did you? By some small grace, she managed to contain the question and all that emerged was a faint, innocuous "Oh."

Why should she be surprised that she didn't understand this man anymore than she understood anyone else? Her faulty judgment was well established, after all. He kissed her, claimed he didn't want to stop kissing her, but was he kissing her *now?*

No. He was staring at her with those heavy-lidded, wrenchingly sexy blue eyes of his, as if he couldn't quite figure out what to do with her.

There was no mystery to solve, as far as she could tell. She was five months' pregnant and had admitted that the baby's father was a slug of a human being.

Why would he want to get involved with that, even if the kiss they'd shared *had* been explosive?

She squelched the pang and the sigh that rose with it, and finally managed to back up a step. Why would she want to get involved, for that matter?

Almost immediately, his hands on hers fell away and she was more convinced than ever that, at last, she was on the right track.

"It's getting dark in here," she said. "I'll light a few candles." And then she'd figure out what to feed them.

The last of the loaf of bread was out. She'd managed to

squash it beyond recognition. It was either eat a meal of raw vegetables—there were plenty still in the fridge—or cook something again over the fire.

She took the matchbook that was sitting on the counter and moved over to the dinette where the trio of candles waited, and struck the match. The flame trembled unsteadily as she set it to the wicks.

Behind her, Darr moved away from the kitchen area. "I'll clean up the game."

She didn't protest but when she heard the wooden clatter of Monopoly houses and hotels sliding into the cardboard box, she closed her eyes against the pang she felt.

After that, the rest of the evening passed in an oddly surreal calm. They shared the hot soup that she heated over the fire, ate peanut butter and saltine crackers, and drank the last of the milk from the refrigerator that was just now beginning to show signs of warming. They heated water in her largest pot to use for washing up—dishes *and* themselves—and he brought in yet more wood from outside while she hid in the candlelit bathroom and prepared for bed, all the while shivering in the cold, tiled room.

They didn't talk about Lyle again.

Or about kissing.

When she came out of the bathroom, he'd unfolded the sofa bed for her, and was tossing the comforter he'd used the night before on top of the cushions he'd situated once again in front of the kitchenette. He'd obviously made himself at home enough to find the blankets and pillows where she kept them in the hall closet.

Strangely enough, she felt no sense of being intruded upon. In fact, there really didn't seem to be anything odd or unusual about his presence at all.

As if he belonged right where he was in the flickering firelight and candlelight.

She chewed the inside of her lip and pulled off the robe that had been a gift from her mother's favored fashion designer, dropped it on the end of the bed and lay down.

And stared blindly up at the ceiling.

"What's wrong?" His voice floated to her, reminding her of the night he'd carried her out of the burning restaurant.

"Nothing." Nothing more than was ever wrong at any rate, and at the moment, even those problems seemed long ago and very far away. She heard the jingle of his belt again. Same as the previous night. The sound of it, too, seemed normal.

Like they were quite the cozy little twosome, together for so long they were as comfortable as old shoes.

Only she'd never felt as if the nerves beneath her skin were ready to burst into song when it came to footwear, a pointed little voice inside her head reminded her.

Beneath the blanket, her stocking-clad toes curled and she reached down and pulled off her socks, folded them up and leaned over to leave them on the side table.

Darr, stripped only down to his jeans and that white T-shirt that hugged his shoulders, was blowing out the candles on the table.

She wondered what he usually wore when he slept.

Pajamas—even just the pants, silk or otherwise—seemed highly unlikely. She lay back down and stared at the ceiling some more, watching the shadows thrown by the fire dance around.

Everything was silent except for the low crackle of the fireplace.

That, and the busyness swirling around inside her head that would not settle down.

She finally turned on her side, scrunched the soft pillow

beneath her neck and looked at the covered mound of him stretched out on the floor. She could clearly make out his tousled hair and the gleam of the white cotton knit clinging to his shoulders.

"Was it still snowing when you went out for the wood?"

"No."

She gnawed at her lip some more. "Do you have a girlfriend?"

He didn't budge. "I jumped your bones in the snow this morning, Bethany. What do you think?"

On one hand, she recognized that he hadn't given a direct answer. On the other hand, she recognized that she believed him anyway. "Were you ever married?"

"No."

"How old are you?"

"Thirty."

"Have you ever come close?"

The comforter finally rustled as he turned on his side to face her. It was too dark to make out the expression in his eyes. She sensed, more than heard, his sigh. "Briefly."

She'd asked the question so she had absolutely no right to feel the pinch inside her at his answer. She moistened her lips. She couldn't seem to make herself drop the matter there, though. "What...what happened?"

"She preferred someone else."

Ouch. She bunched her pillow a little more. "How long ago?"

"Three years."

Which was about how long ago he'd moved to Red Rock, she remembered.

Had he left his heart in California with the woman who'd married someone else? "What was her name?"

He sighed again. "If I tell you, will you go to sleep?"

"Yes."

He made a soft sound. "That didn't really sound convincing, Bethany." There was a faint hint of amusement in his deep voice. "Celia," he added, and the amusement was gone, just like that. "Her name was Celia."

Was she beautiful? This time, Bethany wisely refrained from asking. She didn't know if it was better or worse to have a beautiful name for the faceless woman in his past.

"D'you realize that we've spent more than twenty-four hours together?" Straight. If they'd been seeing one another socially, how many dates would that equal?

"Yeah." Now he just sounded pained. "Do you need something warm to drink? Would that make you sleepier?"

"There's no milk left to warm. There's instant cocoa and water. Do *you* want some?"

In answer, he shoved back the comforter and rummaged around the counter above him. He filled the fire-blackened metal pan with water and took it to the fireplace, then sat on the edge of the brick hearth, watching it heat.

While she watched him.

Around them, the house gave an odd creak and she sat up. "What was that?"

"The house settling, probably." He barely glanced around.

"I wonder how long it'll be before we can get out."

"Tomorrow, one way or another." He retrieved mugs and the envelopes of cocoa mix that he dumped into them and returned to the hearth. Beneath the snug T-shirt, his muscles moved fluidly as he filled the mugs with the quickly heated water and stirred the contents before handing one to her.

She sat up on her elbow to take the mug. Her fingers accidentally brushed his. "Had enough of being cooped up here, then?" She kept her voice light and ducked her head over the hot drink.

"My shift starts tomorrow. Seven in the morning." He'd

made himself a mug of cocoa, too, but she noticed that he didn't drink much of it before he set it on the counter and lowered himself back to his improvised bed.

She sipped, eyeing him over the rim. She supposed if the snow had really stopped that it would quickly start to melt off. But not by seven in the morning. "How will we get your truck out of the snow?"

"I called Nick again when I was bringing in the wood. He'll borrow one of the Double Crown trucks to get here. He'll help get it out."

She fell silent. Of course he wouldn't have just waited around for conditions to improve. He was a take-charge sort of man. She had no reason to feel as if he were abandoning her.

No reason at all.

"I'll get a generator out to you, too, if the electricity isn't restored."

"You don't have to go to all that trouble for me."

"It's no trouble. Probably spend most of my next shift helping people dig out."

She sucked the edge of her lip between her teeth and set aside the mug. "Well…thank you."

"No prob." His comforter rustled and the white gleam of his T-shirt disappeared as he pulled the covers nearly to his ears.

She drew her own blanket to her chin and closed her eyes. She was even *less* sleepy now, but she would pretend to sleep if she had to.

And she would keep her mouth shut.

Darr let out a long, quiet breath when Bethany finally went silent and stayed that way long enough for him to believe she'd mercifully fallen asleep.

She was a pregnant woman. She *needed* her sleep.

He was a man burning up from the inside out and needed something a helluva lot stronger than a powdered hot-chocolate drink to make him forget it.

He threw his arm over his eyes, but nothing could block out her presence just a few feet from him.

And then he heard her voice as she said his name—little more than a whisper above the crackling of the fire—and it put his belief that she'd fallen safely asleep to a grisly death.

If he were a smart man, *he'd* pretend to be asleep. Pretend that he didn't hear that soft, tentative whisper.

Nobody'd ever figured him for genius. "Yeah?"

She was silent for a moment. A log snapped, sending a shower of glowing sparks up the flue. "You'd be warmer on the bed," she finally said.

He exhaled. There was truth in that. A finely honed, double-edged truth. "I'm fine where I am."

He heard her blankets rustle, and in the dim light he saw her push up on her elbow again. Glints of gold and red seemed to reflect off her pale hair. "I don't mind. There's room for us...for us both."

No amount of swallowing was going to combat his arid throat. He finally pushed up on his hands and eyed her. "It's not a good idea."

"Why not?"

He exhaled. "You know why." God in heaven, how could she not?

He couldn't see the expression in her eyes, but he could see the way her lashes fell for a long, silent moment. When they lifted again it felt as if even the fire was holding its breath.

She moved her hand.

And pulled back the covers.

"Bethany—"

"Don't." Her voice was husky. "Don't tell me all the sensible reasons why you think this is not smart."

"If I lay there beside you, I'm going to want to make love to you," he said bluntly. "You realize that?"

She was silent for a heart-thudding minute. "I…I'm not an idiot."

"No. You're a vulnerable, *pregnant,* young woman."

She sat up. Despite the flower-sprigged flannel she wore, he could still see the curve of her shoulder, the taut, full thrust of her breasts, silhouetted against the firelight.

"Does it turn you off? My being pregnant?"

"What'd I just say?" He shoved his fingers through his hair. "God, Bethany. I've been looking for you for weeks. I've wanted you for the last thirty-one freaking hours!"

He could see her lips part. Could hear the indrawn breath she took. Imagined that he could feel the weight of her heart-beat, throbbing in every pulse point.

"I want you, too," she finally said. Quietly. Distinctly. "Don't worry, Darr. I'm not asking for anything more. I just want to be with you. Now. Tonight."

As if he needed any more contributing forces to the erosion of his self-control. The problem was, he was absolutely certain that "now, tonight," wasn't going to be remotely enough for him when it came to Bethany Burdett.

If he were a stronger man, a better man, he'd find some way to talk her off this particular cliff. But he wasn't stronger. He wasn't better.

He wasn't anything but a man who was in a knot over a beautiful woman.

A woman in need.

Dammit. He ought to know better.

He shoved back the blankets that—if he weren't basically

conflagrating from the inside out over her—would be doing a poor job of keeping the encroaching cold at bay, and pushed off the thin couch cushions.

He could feel her gaze on him like a physical thing as he stood beside the sofa bed. "Are you sure?" His voice seemed to come from somewhere deep inside him where there still lingered a kernel of hesitation, of control.

She sat up more fully and with a little shimmy that knotted him right down to his toes, she drew her flannel nightgown up and over her head.

She couldn't have looked more erotic if she'd been doing the Dance of the Seven Veils.

The nightgown seemed to drop, almost in slow motion from her extended fingers, drifting to a soft mound right over his bare toes.

And if that wasn't message enough for his addled soul, which was drinking in the sight of her pink-crested breasts and the curve of her creamy hip as if he'd never seen such a marvel, she held out that hand to him, her fingers trembling ever so slightly. "I'm sure." Her whisper was soft. Throaty.

He closed his hand over her fingers. They felt cool against his palm. He knelt on the mattress and in some graceful dance that he couldn't recall ever learning, he turned her toward him and followed her down, his mouth covering hers.

She tasted of hot chocolate.

And sweet, mindless pleasure.

His pulse raced in his ears, as loud and furious as a firestorm. When he felt her fingertips tug at his rumpled T-shirt, pulling it free of his jeans, and sliding beneath to drift across his abdomen, he nearly came out of his skin.

"Wait." He caught her fingers in his. God help him, but he

was a basket case if just the taste of her lips, the graze of her fingertips, was enough to send him careening out of control.

She stared up at him, her hair an untidy and gut-wrenchingly sexy fan over the pillows around her head. Her breasts rose and fell with her deep, choppy breaths. "You've changed your mind."

He exhaled roughly. "Hell, no." He finished the job of yanking off his shirt himself, and pitched it off the bed to land who knew where. As long as it wasn't in the fire, he didn't care. Then he slid down beside her. "Come here." He pulled her into his arms and she moved smoothly, easily, against him, only to breathe an audible sigh when he rolled back, taking her with him until she was draped over him like the sweetest of blankets.

"Cold?"

"I should be," she whispered. "Considering I'm the naked one here."

Ripe. Naked. Glorious.

But mindful of the undeniable chill in the air, he worked the nubby blanket from beneath his hip and dragged it over the both of them. Beneath, his hands slowly slid up and down her spine, gaining only a few precious inches with each pass.

"You're making me crazy." Her words were little more than a whisper that burned along his jaw. Her knees slid to either side of his hips and she sat up, bracing her hand flat against his abdomen.

He lifted his head and caught one of those taunting, tempting nipples between his lips.

She made a soft sound. A needy purr of a sound that drove him mad. But when she reached for the waist of his jeans, he sucked in a hard breath, his head falling back. She popped open the button. And then another. Slowly. Tormenting.

He muttered an oath and yanked apart the rest of his fly, shoving the jeans away. "Come here." He pulled her back to him, and nearly cried like a baby when her hand snuck between them, circling him. Her thigh slid over his hips and in one smooth arch, she suddenly took him in. Fully. Completely.

He very nearly forgot how to breathe.

He damn sure forgot everything he'd ever known about self-control.

"I can't wait," she whispered thickly. "I'm sorry. I've never wanted anyone so badly."

He caught her hips in his hands, holding her tight. Still. But deep inside her, where she held him so intimately gloved, he could feel the very pulse of her. "You think that requires an apology?"

She lowered her mouth toward his. "Kiss me." Her whisper teased his lips. "Kiss me like you never want to stop."

The problem was he *didn't* ever want to stop.

The problem was, in the cold light of day, he figured *she* would.

His hands swept up her spine, slid over her tumbled hair and cradled her face while his mouth caught hers. And then there was just too damn much sensation to think about problems or what the next morning would bring, or even what the next hour would bring.

All he cared about was the moment.

The slide of her tongue against his.

The press of her fingertips against his ribs.

The soft cries that rose in her throat as they rocked together, as perfectly attuned as two lovers had ever been, and the fluttering, grasping spasms deep inside her that clutched him, drugged him, maddened him. And when she gasped his name and threw her head back, every line of her taut body shining in the firelight, he practically felt the top of his head blow off as he spun along with her, emptying everything he was inside her.

And then all was still.

Except for those sweet, nearly painful aftershocks working through her as her head dropped forward and she slowly collapsed against him.

His heart felt like a freight train inside his head. Her breathing was more like a marathoner's gasps. Despite the pervasive chill in the room, they were both slick with sweat. His hands were actually shaking when he closed them over her spine. "I didn't hurt you, did I?"

She pressed her forehead more tightly into the curve of his neck. Shook her head. "It…you…were perfect."

She'd drained everything out of him. He felt about as macho as a weak kitten who'd been run down by a hurricane. "Honey, there ain't a man alive who wouldn't want to take the credit when a woman tells him that, but you were the perfect one."

"It wasn't me." She lifted her tousled head. In the firelight, her eyes were dark, gleaming pools. She slid her hand over his still-racing heart. "I've never felt anything like that before. Not ever."

"Well, gee. Thanks, ma'am," he drawled after the too-long pause his addled brain took to absorb that. "Glad to be of service."

She gave a half laugh, and pressed her forehead to his shoulder again. "The aw-shucks tone isn't quite believable coming from you."

He grinned into the dark and smoothly turned her onto her back. The slight thrust of her belly was visible in the flickering glow. As were the pink nipples that tightened even more as he looked at her. "Good. But when I finish making you crazy again, you'll see that I'm not exaggerating about the service part." He ran his hand over her waist. Splayed his fingers over the burgeoning swell of her baby.

She caught her breath, and pressed her hands against his, stilling his motion. "Feel that?"

He felt plenty. The satiny warmth of her skin. The indentation of her navel beneath his thumb. The downy mound beneath his little finger. The desire rising inside him again, as if he were fifteen instead of thirty.

"That's the baby moving," she prompted.

His attention abruptly pinpointed to the firm swell under his palm. "Seriously?"

"Wait," she whispered. "There." In a flash, she pressed their hands about an inch to the right.

And he did feel it.

The faintest of small flutters. Like the wings of a butterfly scraping against his palm. "Jesus," he breathed. He slid around until his face was right next to her belly. "Hey there, peanut," he said against her. "How's it going?"

She laughed softly and lifted one hand, sliding it slowly through his hair. "You're the nut."

"So I've been told." He probably was. Just then, he didn't give a flip.

He pressed his lips to her abdomen and she caught her breath. Her fingers tightened. "Darr."

Not a protest. Just a sigh of his name.

He closed his eyes. Wondered if he was imagining the flutter of the baby that he felt against his lips and decided that it didn't matter. The baby was there and he couldn't ignore it anymore than he could ignore the idea that had started swimming inside of him hours earlier.

Long before she'd seduced him into sharing the bed.

"Marry me," he said.

Chapter Seven

Bethany stiffened. "What?"

He sat up and despite the cold douse of shock coursing through her, she couldn't help but appreciate the thoroughly masculine beauty of him. "I know it sounds crazy," he admitted, "but it makes perfect sense."

"Why? Just because we slept together?" She didn't believe for a minute that any man in this present day and age would think one should necessitate the other.

"If you need a reason, yeah. Because we slept together."

"No. No. You don't want to marry me," she countered swiftly, denying the very idea of it. For pity's sake, she'd practically had to beg him to make love to her. "It's not like you need to rescue my virtue." Her parents had essentially auctioned that off to Lyle, though Darr had no way of knowing that.

He exhaled briefly, impatiently. "This isn't a rescue."

"Of course it is. And I need to take care of myself. All my

life I've let other people do that, and look what happened!"
She spread her fingers across the swell of her baby.

His gaze followed her hands and she couldn't help but
swallow hard when she saw the way his gaze drifted upward,
lingering on her breasts. Nor could she help the way her flesh
tightened, the way her nipples pebbled and rose like they
were begging for his attention.

They *were* begging, darn it all.

Every nerve in her body wanted more of his touch.

More of him.

"As my wife, you would be immediately covered under my
insurance." His voice was a hair ragged and she felt a per-
versely feminine thrill over it. "So would the baby. I'm hardly
rolling in dough, but I can still provide. We could find a
house here in Red Rock. Or even build. You wouldn't have
to work unless you chose to. And you damn sure wouldn't
have to worry about that spineless bastard finding you.
You…and the baby…would have my name." His angled jaw
looked carved from stone. "Nobody messes with a Fortune
and gets away with it."

What he offered sounded so easy. So plausible. So reasonable.

"We hardly know each other!"

"We know enough."

That was the problem. He didn't know enough. And she
couldn't bring herself to tell him.

What would he think when he learned how little she'd
truly mattered to her own family? That they'd rather marry her
off to an abuser than give up the millions that Lyle had been
prepared to invest in the family business upon their marriage?

Maybe Darr would end up agreeing.

Her small gains of independence were too fresh, too tender

to put to the test. If she backslid now, what would happen later when it wasn't just her pregnant self she had to take care of, but a tiny, defenseless baby, as well?

"I can't marry you."

"You mean you won't."

She slid off the bed and stood. "I mean I can't! You're a nice man, Darr. A decent man." Her gaze caught. An aroused man. "A…a really…decent man," she repeated doggedly. Goose bumps that had nothing to do with the chill in the air were dancing down her spine, and she snatched up her robe, dragging it over her shoulders.

The velvet felt excruciatingly soft against her hypersensitive skin.

His calloused fingertips had felt even better.

She dragged the belt around her waist and yanked it into a knot. If only she could tie up and put away her reaction to him just as decisively.

"And it's not that I don't appreciate your noble intentions, but truly, they're not necessary. I have to take care of myself." If she didn't do it now, she feared that she never would.

"And I'm telling you that you don't have to do it alone."

Maybe later, when she had reason to have more faith in herself, she could afford to let herself think that way. But not now. Not yet.

Not even if the offer of help came gift-wrapped in the altogether addictive appeal of Darr Fortune.

"I just—" She broke off when the house seemed to groan again. More loudly than before.

Even Darr stood. His eyes narrowed in concentration. Then he suddenly swore and snatched up his jeans.

She'd never seen anyone dress so fast. From two T-shirts to boots. "What's—"

But he'd already grabbed his coat and was heading out the door. "Stay inside." The order was terse.

The groaning turned into a high-pitched screech as he closed the door behind him and she nearly jumped out of her skin.

She hopped around tugging on her socks and pushing her feet into her tennis shoes, showing absolutely none of the finesse or efficiency that Darr had exhibited. Getting her coat was too much effort so she just grabbed the blanket off the tumbled bed, threw it around her shoulders and dashed out after him.

The cold air hit her like a fist, and the soles of her shoes slid on the steps.

She grabbed the handrail to keep from flying head over heels and paused, willing her heart back into place. She had the baby to consider! She needed to be more careful.

Another screech squealed eerily and she quickly moved off the steps. Her tennis shoes broke the crisp surface of snow and she sank down to her ankles.

"Dammit, Bethany, I told you to stay inside." Darr's voice came from several yards away and she focused on the darker shadow of his form barely visible in the thin moonlight and headed toward him. He was some distance from the side of the house, facing it.

"I don't like being told what to do."

"Then use your common sense. You don't need to be out here catching a cold." His arm came up, holding her back when she reached him. "Far enough."

She hitched the blanket higher around her shoulders and clutched it at her waist to keep it from dragging in the snow. "Is it the roof?" She hoped it wasn't, but assumed that if it were, the owners would have to fix it.

"Carport," Darr said, and swore when yet another screech rent the air, followed by a gunshot of a crack.

Bethany nearly screamed, she was so startled, and Darr pulled her close, turning his back toward the house even as an explosive crash vibrated right through their feet. Chunks of snow flew out at them, raining over their heads.

And then there was nothing but awful, horrible, silence.

"I should've known," he muttered finally, holding her tightly. His hand brushed over her head. Her shoulders. "Are you hurt?"

She shook her head and looked up. "What—" Her throat clamped shut with horror. "My car," finally emerged, sounding strangled.

Even in the dark she could make out the scene. Could see the tumble of debris from what had *been* the carport, along with a massive pile of snow, now smashed squarely down on the hood of her car.

Her caved-in car, that was.

"Don't try to get closer to it." Darr's hands closed around her again when she started toward it. "There's still one post holding up the backside of the roof, but the structure's too unstable."

She blinked back the sudden burning in her eyes. "I can't believe this is happening." It had taken her weeks to find a car she could afford, and a seller who didn't look too closely at her personal information.

How was she supposed to get around now? To work? To her obstetrician's appointments?

"Insurance should cover it."

She was twenty-five years old. She should know how things like insurance worked! And wasn't that one of the very points she'd been making only a few minutes ago?

She flopped her hands. The blanket fell off her shoulders but she hardly noticed. She had no idea how long a process it would be to get the vehicle fixed. If it could be fixed. And if it couldn't, what then? "What if it doesn't?"

"We'll figure something out."

"This is not your problem, Darr. *I* am not your problem!"

"Maybe I don't look at you and see a *problem*," he countered quietly. He turned her toward him again, snuggling the blanket once more up around her shoulders, and slipped his hand beneath her chin until she couldn't do anything but look at him. "I can *help* you, Bethany. I want to. This is all the more reason to marry me."

Her jaw set. "I've already told you no."

"You're not even going to consider it."

If she did, she'd probably cave in and agree, that's how weak she was. "There's nothing to consider," she insisted.

"You're a damn stubborn woman, you know that?"

Nobody had ever accused her of that, but she realized she much preferred stubborn over weak.

She shivered and hitched the blanket up to cover her chin and turned to eye the remains of her car. Once it was daylight, she feared the mess would look even worse.

Belatedly, it occurred to her that the mess could have been *far* worse. Several times, Darr had stood under that carport splitting wood. What if it had come down on *him?*

She felt sick at the thought. "Better the car than you."

"True. Come on. There's nothing we can do out here in the dark. You're freezing. Let's get inside."

"Do you think the house is safe?"

"The carport was definitely added after the house was built." He pointed. "See? It's separated completely from the exterior wall."

That was at least one positive note.

She headed back toward the porch. Each step she took had her shoes cracking through the snow and by the time they made it inside, there was snow caked inside the shoes, packed and freezing, all around her heels.

She peeled out of them, and her socks, and sat down on the side of the bed, rubbing her feet with the end of her blanket, drying and trying to warm them.

Darr left his boots by the door as usual and dropped his jacket over the back of a chair. With no hint of the self-consciousness that was presently plaguing her, he flipped his shirts off over his head and tugged off his socks, then shucked his jeans.

She lowered her gaze to her feet, but couldn't help peeking through her lashes as he moved around, naked as the day his mama had brought him into the world, and a whole lot more grown up. He spread his jeans across the hearth, close enough to absorb the heat but still a safe distance from the unscreened flame.

Then he stepped in front of her and crouched low, covering her cold feet with his hands and rubbing gently. "Take off your robe."

Heat streaked through her veins.

"It's wet from the snow," he added. "You don't want to get the bed wet, too."

Her hormones didn't come to a jolting stop, but they should have. "Right." Feeling even more self-conscious, she slid the robe off her shoulders.

It was one thing to strip down to nothing but skin when you were making love. It was another thing to do so when the guy rubbing sensation back into your feet was just being practical.

But he hardly seemed to look at her anyway as he grabbed the comforter from the cushions on the floor and dumped it in her lap before spreading the long folds of the robe over the side chair so it, too, would dry. Then he tossed the pillow that he'd been using onto the bed and gestured. "Scoot over."

She hesitated. "Um—"

"It's probably twenty degrees outside and the only wood we've got to get us through the night that's not buried under that carport is that stack there." He gestured at the small pile of split logs that still remained. "We're both cold. We'll be warmer in bed. Together."

She felt tongue-tied with desire for the man she'd insisted she wouldn't marry. And he *was* merely being practical.

Again.

She reached for the flannel nightgown that she'd pulled off so wantonly not all that much earlier and yanked it over her head, not much caring if he thought she was being silly or not.

With a snap, she flipped out the comforter so it spread across the bed and, without looking at him, slipped into bed beneath it. Facing the kitchenette kept her back to "his" side of the bed and she shoved her pillow under her head, pulling the comforter up to her ears.

Fortunately, he didn't say a word.

The bedsprings creaked as he joined her on the thin mattress and she tried not to be excruciatingly aware of the tiny points of contact he made along her spine as he settled himself.

He was still for only a few tight moments before he shifted again, with another creak of bedsprings.

Odd how she hadn't noticed that squeaking when they'd been giving the ancient bed a considerably more vigorous workout.

He made a muffled sound. "The floor's almost better than this thing. How do you manage to sleep?"

Defensiveness hunched her shoulders. "You weren't complaining earlier."

"We weren't sleeping earlier," he reminded her pointedly. Needlessly.

She closed her eyes, which only served to bring the still-vivid sensations he'd wrought from her into sharper focus. Making love with Darr was so completely different than her experience with Lyle had been. Then she'd just been anxious to get it over with.

Now with Darr, her insides felt liquefied, wanting only to relive the experience.

Again. And again.

She shoved aside the comforter.

"What's wrong?"

"Nothing." She pushed off the bed and went into the bathroom, closing the door behind her. It was dark as pitch inside with no electricity or candles or firelight, the tile even more uncomfortably cold against her bare feet, but that didn't stop her from accomplishing the necessary, and with her bladder happy once again, she hurried back to the warmth of the bed.

She was trying to keep the folds of her nightgown down around her calves, keep the comforter up around her ears, and find a comfortable position when Darr sighed. "*What* are you doing?"

"My nightgown's tangled."

"Then take it off." His tone was short. And it was certainly devoid of seductive suggestion.

"I don't think so." She yanked the fabric until it was straight again and well below her knees, and pushed the pillow more comfortably beneath her head.

"You need a decent bed."

"Well, this is the only bed I have."

"*I* have a very comfortable king-size bed."

"You have my heartiest congratulations."

"I don't know why you're sounding so ticked off. I'm the one who's had his proposal tossed back in his face."

Her jaws ached. "You only offered out of pity."

"The only thing I pity is our backs from the freaking springs poking through this joke of a mattress."

She stared at the dancing gleam of the fire reflecting against the metal legs of the dinette set.

Between Darr and her car, her thoughts were so jumbled that she wasn't sure she'd ever sleep.

"If I said yes—" which she had absolutely no intention of doing "—what would *you* get out of it?"

"Honey, you have got to be kidding me." His voice was arid.

Her lips twisted. She was getting bigger by the week. "Wait a month and see if you still feel remotely interested."

His arm suddenly scooped around her waist and he slid her smoothly, easily, across the space that separated them.

The surprised gasp that rose in her throat got strangled before it could even emerge when he gripped her hip and tucked her bottom snugly against him.

"Does that feel remote?"

There was no mistaking his meaning.

He was hard. Rock hard. And no amount of thin, cheap flannel between them could have hidden it.

Her paltry shore of resistance was no match for the torrent of want that swamped her. "Darr."

His fingertips flexed against her hip and for an infinitesimal moment, he pressed harder against her. "Don't worry. Evidence to the contrary, I do have some self-control. Go to sleep."

Maybe he had self-control, but she didn't. She wished that she hadn't been so set on wearing the nightgown. That she could feel his hair-roughened chest against her back and his long legs twining with hers. That his hand would slide up, over her aching breasts, or down, between her legs.

That he'd bring her again to that overwhelming, all-encompassing ecstasy that—until him, *with* him—she'd always believed was a wildly exaggerated myth.

She pressed her wrist against her mouth and remained painfully still despite the yearning inside her that imagined arching against him, savoring the magical differences between her body and his.

Eventually, his absolute calmness started to penetrate, though, and instead of bracing against her own thundering pulse, she began to feel the steady beat of his. Her short breaths found—and followed—the pace of his slower, easier ones.

And at last, without even being aware of when it happened, her muscles relaxed into the too-thin mattress, and she slept.

The next thing she knew, daylight was filling the room, creeping easily beyond the thin curtain at the window, and Darr was nowhere to be found.

She could, however, hear deep voices coming from outside. Maybe that was what had woken her.

Or maybe it was the baby pressing on her bladder again.

The alarm clock that sat on the side table was still dark, which meant the electricity was still out. She quickly climbed out of bed, visited the bathroom that was not quite as cold as it had been the night before, and went to the window to look out.

The sky was pale blue and clear with not a cloud in sight, and the horizon was lined with gold from the rising sun. It looked like a perfectly lovely day in the making.

Except that she was still surrounded by snow, the electricity was still out, and her car was still flat.

Still. Still. Still.

She exhaled, and her breath made a faint cloud against the cold windowpane.

A large white pickup truck was parked near Darr's, which had been wiped clean of snow. He and another man—presumably his brother, Nick—were wielding wide, flattish snow shovels as they cleared a track, from where it was mired in snow, to the road.

It was obviously warmer outside. Both men's heads were bare, and Darr's leather jacket wasn't even zipped up.

She nibbled the inside of her lip. At least one of them would be able to get to work.

She, however, would need to get in touch with the owners of the house about the collapsed carport, and figure out what to do about her car.

The fire was burned down to a red glow and there were no more pieces of wood stacked against the wall. Darr must have continued feeding the fire while she'd slept.

The baby jittered around inside her and she pressed her hand to her side. "I know," she murmured aloud. "He's something, isn't he?"

When she saw the two men jam their shovel blades into the ridge of snow they'd created alongside the clearing and turn toward the house, she quickly stepped away from the window. Snatching fresh clothes from the drawer, she darted into the bathroom.

When she came out again, dressed and as presentable as she could make herself, given the lack of warm water and electricity, the door was just opening.

Darr spotted her standing in the hallway immediately, of course. Since he'd arrived on her doorstep Friday afternoon, the dark shadow of beard had deepened across his angular jaw.

It just made him look that much more masculine. That much more dangerous to her shaky emotions.

"Good. You're awake." He gestured behind him, and pushed the door wider. "Come on in, Nick."

Bethany brushed her hands self-consciously down the front of her brown corduroys. She didn't suppose it had occurred to Darr that she might feel awkward with a stranger coming into her house while the bed they'd shared was still unfolded and noticeably tumbled.

She didn't know if it was ironic or not that she no longer categorized Darr as a stranger. No matter how briefly you'd known someone, she supposed that's what happened when you lived in each other's pockets for a couple of nights, made love like you were the last two people on earth and argued over a well-intentioned, albeit loveless, marriage proposal.

"Hello, Mr. Fortune." She stepped forward with her hand outstretched, ignoring the bed and the memory of all that had occurred there, when Darr's brother stepped inside and closed the door behind him. "I'm Barbara Burton. Nice to meet Darr's rescue crew." She didn't realize until she introduced herself that it hadn't occurred to her that Darr might have told his brother her real name.

Even with his shoulders padded with a thick, downy coat, it was obvious that Nicholas Fortune was slightly leaner than Darr. He was also a few inches taller. But there was definitely a similarity in the way the corner of his lips kicked up as he stepped forward to close her hand in a brief, businesslike grip. "Mr. Fortune's our dad," he said, sounding vaguely amused. "Make it Nick. Nice to meet you, too. Bet you'll be glad to get rid of this guy." He gave Darr a clap on the shoulder.

Would she be rid of him?

Now that the snowstorm looked like it was finally over, would he realize the folly of his proposal?

A quick glance toward his impassive face told her nothing. "I was glad not to be alone. Your brother's been very helpful," she demurred.

"He's good at that." Unlike Darr, Nick's eyes were brown. And openly curious as they went from Bethany to Darr and back again. "The Foundation office is closed today, just in case you were worrying about that."

Which meant that Darr had told Nick that she worked there, because she highly doubted that the man would be aware of it otherwise. They had never even met. "That's good to know."

The extra day would give her a little bit more time to solve the matter of transportation. She didn't want to use a taxi service and no bus line ran to her neighborhood. A bicycle would be fine if the road was clear of snow, but only temporarily because she just couldn't see herself riding down that hill when she was nine months' pregnant.

"Here." Darr held out his truck keys toward her, almost as if he'd read her mind. "We've shoveled a healthy path. Don't go forward or you might get stuck again. But you'll be able to back straight out to the street. A plow came through just after dawn."

She stared at the keys. "Excuse me?"

"Nick's gonna drop me at the firehouse," he continued. "I'll be on duty for the next twenty-four hours. Longer if I have to pull a double."

"Darr, I can't take your truck!"

"Well, you can't drive your car," he returned evenly. When she still didn't take the keys, he tossed them onto the table. "I called the power company. Electricity's supposed to be restored by midmorning to all of Red Rock. If yours isn't, call me. Use the cell number, not the main line for the firehouse. The guy who usually answers the phone there can't write a message for diddly. It's on the card I gave you. You might have to leave a voice mail but I'll get back to you as quickly as I càn."

Before she could get in a word edgewise, he leaned down and planted a hard kiss on her lips.

"I did mean what I said," he told her when he lifted his head. "Think about it."

Bethany didn't say anything when he opened the door and preceded his brother—whose gaze was now even more speculative—outside.

She was too busy keeping her knees from dissolving beneath her.

Chapter Eight

"Think about what?" Nick barely waited until they were in the cab of the truck he'd borrowed from Lily's ranch before he fired the question.

"Nothing you need to worry about." Darr fastened his seat belt as the powerful truck—complete with chains on the tires—reversed over the clearing they'd made.

"Yeah, that helps," Nick drawled. "You went there and burned the sheets with her, didn't you?"

Since Darr considered that to be his business, he didn't answer that, either.

"Well." Nick turned the wheel and started heading down the gravel hill. "Can't say I blame you there. The girl's a looker."

"And too young for the likes of you."

"Got your protective instincts going, has she?" Nick laughed softly and Darr wished he'd kept his mouth shut.

"Don't sweat it," Nick said. "Frankly, I'm glad you're finally acting normal again."

"Hold up. Stop here," Darr said when they neared the side street and John Decker's house on the corner.

Nick obediently braked and Darr quickly hopped out and left the borrowed gloves tucked inside the old man's mailbox. There was nothing he could do about the axe at the moment, since it was buried beneath Bethany's pancaked carport. A trip to the hardware store would fix that quickly enough, though. "What do you mean, normal?" he asked, the second he climbed back in the truck.

"You know. Going out. Romancing the ladies," Nick continued the second Darr climbed back in the truck. "Having some fun, you know?"

"I'm going to marry her."

Nick slammed on the brakes again and the truck fishtailed to a drunken stop. Nick looped his arm over the steering wheel and stared at Darr. "Say again?"

Darr's jaw tightened. "You heard me."

"You proposed. You know the woman for two days and you propose." Nick looked out the windshield, as if he were trying to fathom the unfathomable. Then his sharp gaze shot right back to Nick. "Are you out of your mind?"

Darr stared back, unflinching.

"*Why?* That's taking Valentine's Day to the extreme, don't you think?"

The truth was, Darr hadn't given the holiday another thought after he'd climbed into bed beside Bethany. "Could we go now, or do you want to sit here until all the snow thaws?"

Nick, however, didn't put the truck in gear. "You know, you *can* sleep with a woman these days without going down on bended knee. I doubt anyone's going to come running for you with shotgun in hand."

"This has nothing to do with sleeping with her." And he was annoyed with himself for letting his brother egg him into admitting it.

Particularly when he could see Nick's brain ticking behind his glasses. "Oh, hell," his brother said, looking suddenly resigned. "You're trying to rescue her. That's it, isn't it? Just like you tried with Celia."

"Dammit, Nick. Leave it alone."

"Ahh." Nick rolled his head around on his shoulders as he swore more ripely. "Anyone ever tell you that you have an overabundance of conscience? Darwin. *Dude*. You don't have to make up for the rest of society's failures when it comes to some poor woman!" He shot Darr another look. "So what's her story? Grew up in poverty? Got knocked around by a drunk parent? A scumbag boyfriend?" His eyes sharpened. "That's it. I can see it in your eyes. You want to keep her from going back to the guy who beat her."

"Do you want me to *walk* back to the firehouse?" He flipped off his seat belt and reached for the door in one rapid motion.

Nick sighed noisily. "Don't be so touchy. You're the one going around proposing to complete strangers. You expect me to just whip out the attaboys over it?"

"She's not a stranger."

"Because you've been in her pants?"

"Dammit, Nick, shut the hell up!"

Surprisingly, his brother did. Nick watched him, his thumb slowly tapping the steering wheel. "Look, I get it that marriage isn't anathema to you like it is to…well, to me. But I just don't want to see you tearing yourself up again like you did before," Nick finally said quietly.

"This is not about Celia." Darr's voice was tight.

"Are you sure?"

Darr stared out the window but in his mind, all he saw was Bethany's small house and the collapsed carport.

Was he sure?

He'd slept with Celia. When they were high school sweethearts, bent more on a good time than ever after. But when they'd graduated, she'd gone her way and he'd gone his.

And he hadn't seen her again until they'd been called out on a domestic disturbance.

The guy in question had needed his shoulder sewn up after slamming it through a window before the cops could haul him in. The pregnant girl in question had needed sobering up and several months' worth of good meals.

Celia.

He'd made sure she was fed. Got her to the doctor for some very tardy prenatal care. Gave her a shoulder to lean on when she'd needed it, and done everything he could to help her get back on her feet. And when she'd begged him to keep the baby's father from trying to take the baby from her after he was born, Darr had agreed to help then, too. She was a friend. A girl he'd once cared about.

So they decided that marriage was the best course. But he'd never loved her.

And when she'd gone back to the jerk anyway, Darr hadn't done anything to stop her.

A week after that, both she and her baby were dead and not even the fact that the bastard who'd done it was rotting in jail mitigated Darr's sense of having failed to act when he could have.

He knew if he told Nick that Bethany was pregnant, his brother would be more convinced than ever that he was trying to relive—and rewrite—the past.

Telling Nick that he was in love with Bethany wouldn't get him anywhere, either.

It was hard enough to believe it himself.

And if he'd added that particular point to Bethany, he figured she'd disappear for good the second he turned his back.

"I suppose she agreed," Nick finally said when Darr remained silent. Then rolled his eyes. "What the hell. You're a Fortune. Of course she agreed."

"Just tell me what else happened out at the Double Crown," Darr answered instead. "And do it on the way to the firehouse."

Mercifully, Nick put the vehicle in gear and headed back down the street and toward town. "Not much. Lily plays a mean hand of poker. She even gave Dad a run for his money. Aunt Cindy got hold of Ross. She says he agreed to look into the notes."

"One of the Fortunes isn't who we think," Darr recounted.

"Pretty much."

"Sounds like a bunch of bull to me." The only person Darr knew who wasn't who people thought was Bethany. And she had good reason to disguise her identity.

"Bull or not, Ross should be able to get to the bottom of it," Nick said. "Nobody threatens a Fortune and gets away with it."

Which is exactly what Darr had told Bethany.

That hadn't convinced her to marry him anymore than anything else had.

He exhaled. He could be patient when he had to be. And persistent.

She'd change her mind.

It was the lack of milk that got Bethany out of the house later that afternoon.

She approached Darr's truck, with his keys clutched in her

hands, as if it were about to rear up its chrome grill like some menacing snout and strike.

She'd contacted the house owners in San Antonio about the carport. They'd promised to contact their insurance agent, who promised to send someone out to review the situation.

She'd contacted representatives of the insurance company about her car. They'd promised to send someone out to review the situation.

She'd even contacted the folks at the utility company about her continued lack of electricity, and they'd admitted that most of the town's service had been restored. And *they'd* promised to send someone out to review the situation.

Well, she'd reviewed the situation in her warm refrigerator, when her stomach wouldn't stop growling, and determined that it was time for her to take action.

Which meant taking Darr's truck.

The sun was well up in the sky and all around her the snow was melting at a furious pace, as if it wanted to retreat just as rapidly as it had unexpectedly struck. In fact, the temperature was so pleasant that she wore only a long-sleeved blouse beneath her unbuttoned peacoat, and when she braved climbing behind the wheel of Darr's truck and had figured out enough of the fancy controls, she turned off the heat and rolled the windows halfway down to enjoy the afternoon air.

She was almost giddy with gratitude that the truck had an automatic transmission. It was bad enough that she'd never driven such a large vehicle in her life; if it had been a stick shift, she'd have been just as stuck as if Darr hadn't left the truck for her to use at all.

The pretty little BMWs that her father had been bestowing upon her every other birthday since she'd turned sixteen had all but driven themselves.

Her lips firmed. Maybe if he'd been less extravagant with unnecessary cars for her, he wouldn't have tried selling her off to the man who was supposed to save their business.

She craned her neck around and slowly backed the truck across the wide yard toward the street. She probably could have managed to turn it around in a circle with the way the snow was melting, but she didn't want to take a chance when it was Darr's property she was borrowing.

Relief sighed through her when, still in reverse, she bumped safely over the curb and turned to head straight down the gravel hill.

John Decker was in his yard and she waved her hand at him as she passed. Not surprisingly, he did not return the greeting.

There were lots of people out in their yards as she drove toward the center of town. Adults shoveling sidewalks. Kids playing in the melting banks of snow. She knew if she turned down Main, she would pass the firehouse, and the urge to do so was strong.

No matter how vigorously she refused to entertain the notion of marrying Darr Fortune, she couldn't deny the part of her that wanted to debate the matter.

She'd been truthful when she'd told Darr's brother that she'd been glad he was there during the storm.

But that didn't mean they should go turning one weekend of unusual extremes into something it wasn't. So she would just have to get her fascination as far as Darr was concerned under control before she ruined things altogether.

Her hands tightened around the steering wheel as she turned in the opposite direction and tried focusing on the matter at hand.

There was no point in trying to entirely restock her refrigerator yet. For one thing, she didn't have that much cash, and for another, an electric refrigerator without electricity was as useless as no refrigerator at all. She'd wait until that matter was resolved, and then she'd find a way to get to San Antonio and the big-box discount stores there where the prices would be easier on her wallet.

Instead, she wandered the aisles of the hardware store until she found a small, inexpensive ice chest, then went to the grocery store and bought a half gallon of milk and a few other essentials that would keep her going for a few days. In the parking lot, she dumped a bag of ice cubes around the milk inside the cooler, fit the top in place, and lifted it to the passenger side floor of the truck.

"Darr, is that you?"

Bethany lifted her head with a start, staring across at the tall, curvaceous redhead who stood on the other side of the truck. "Nope. Sorry."

The woman's brows quirked together. "Sorry, too. I thought this was someone else's truck." She smiled brightly, though there was a questioning crinkle between her brows. "You look familiar. Have I seen you around Red Rock before?"

Bethany returned the smile noncommittally. "No. I don't think so." She tucked her other two bags beside the cooler and shut the door, rounding the front of the truck.

The other woman stood taller than her by half a foot, which put Bethany's head right about level with a truly impressive bosom when the other woman didn't move away from the driver's side door. "Oh. Excuse me." The woman quickly shifted so Bethany could reach the door. "I'm Lorena Evans," she introduced.

"Barbara Burton," Bethany returned. She pulled open Darr's door and reached her foot up for the high running board.

"Are you new or just passing through?"

Bethany couldn't bring herself to be rude. Red Rock was her home. At least for now, and the residents there were her neighbors. "New."

"Well, we sure put on the fine weather for you then, didn't we?" Lorena grinned ruefully. "I work at SusieMae's down on Main. Best meal you can find in town, at least until Red's back up and running." She leaned forward. "But don't tell SusieMae I said that," she added with hushed humor.

"Your secret's safe with me. I'd better go and get this stuff home."

Lorena backed away with an easy smile. "Nice t'meet you."

"You, too." Bethany pulled the door shut and started the engine. A moment later, still feeling strange sitting so high up in the truck, she drove carefully out of the small parking lot. She was quite satisfied with herself by the time she made it back to the house, and parked the truck in the same spot where Darr had left it.

There were more bare patches of ground visible now, but the melting snow also meant water and, in her yard, that particular combination meant mud. Better to stick to the area where the snow had been cleared.

The phone was ringing stridently when she carried her purchases inside. The sound was so unfamiliar that she was reluctant to answer it. But she'd made a lot of calls that morning, and some of them would no doubt result in returned calls.

So she picked up.

"Are you all right?" Darr's voice was unmistakable, though there was a loud, constant roar behind it.

"Fine." She pulled her purse off her shoulder and dropped it onto the couch that she'd restored to order after he and Nick had left that morning.

"I've been calling for the past hour."

"Oh." She moistened her lips. It wasn't demand that was in his voice. If it had been, she'd have felt no compunction whatsoever in telling him what he could do with it.

She'd had enough of *that* with Lyle.

But it was concern that she heard, and against that, it seemed she had few defenses. "I went to the store to buy a few things."

"Your electricity's back on then?"

"Well, no. Not yet."

"Hold on." She heard him speaking, muffled, to someone else, and then he came back. And still there was that noise in the background.

"Where are you?"

"On the engine. Heading back to the firehouse. We've been responding to calls all day. It's been pretty crazy."

"You're all decked out in your uniform then."

"Turnouts." He sounded amused, suddenly. "Yes, ma'am. If that image does it for you, maybe we should talk about that…thing…again."

That *thing* meant his marriage proposal, she knew, but she still couldn't help the flush that ran right down her body. "There's nothing to talk about," she said primly. "And I wouldn't have thought you'd be allowed to make personal calls while you're on duty."

He laughed out loud at that, and the strength seemed to leave her knees in a rush. She sat down on the couch with an inelegant plop. "My Cap is sitting next to me," he told her. "He saw me dialing so I guess I must be okay. I'd tell you that you can come stay at my place—I know for a fact the apartment building's got electricity—but I suppose you'll turn that down, too."

Of all the things they'd talked about over the weekend, the

only thing she knew about his home was that he rarely used his own television. And she couldn't pretend that she wasn't curious about where he lived.

A useless curiosity, she reminded herself firmly.

"I called the utility company," she told him. "They said they'll send someone to check it out."

"Good. I'll call you later. See how it's going."

"Darr, that's really not neces—"

"Gotta go," he said cheerfully, and disconnected.

Bethany held the phone out from her ear, staring at it when the background noise of the fire engine was replaced by the low drone of the dial tone. Thoroughly bemused, she leaned over and replaced the receiver.

True to his word, he called again later.

This time, she was outside dealing with the insurance adjuster that the owners had arranged.

The good news was the damage would be covered, and the carport would be replaced.

The bad news was only the damage to the actual carport was covered.

Her car was another matter.

She was heading into the house when she heard the phone ringing and nearly vaulted over the coffee table to reach it, but it stopped before she got there.

She knew it was Darr, though.

Who else was calling her these days?

The third time he called, it was nighttime and she was sound asleep in bed, and the strident ringing nearly sent her nerves right through the roof. Which is what she deserved for setting the phone on the mattress right beside her pillow.

"Third time's a charm," she said in greeting.

"Sorry I woke you."

She brushed her hair out of her eyes and turned to face the side of the bed that he'd occupied the night before. "How do you know I was sleeping?"

"I can hear it in your voice. You've got power going?

"Mmm-hmm. Thanks for that, too." Even now she could hear the hum of the generator that had been delivered and hooked up by the three very capable and very good-looking off-duty firefighters sent by Darr shortly before dark. "How did you know my electricity still hadn't been restored?"

"I have my connections. They show you how it works before they left?"

"Yes. Your friends were very helpful and thorough."

"Joe and Marcus are both married," he said. "Don't pay any attention to their flirting."

She bit back a smile, but then let it loose since he couldn't see it anyway. "And Rick?"

"Big-time social problems. He's seriously afraid of women."

Laughter bubbled in her throat. "He is not." The tallest of the three, Rick had talked of nothing but his sweetheart. "His girlfriend's name is Elise and she's an elementary school teacher."

"Yeah, okay. You caught me."

She hadn't really, though. He was just putting on the unexpected charm to sway her to his way of thinking.

"I don't know how I'll repay you for the generator, but I will."

"I'm not looking for repayment. The generator's from the Double Crown. You can thank Lily when you meet her. And if you think I arranged it so you'd feel obliged to marry me, you're way off track. And no, I don't want your apology if that's what you're trying to come up with."

She had been. "All right. But I'm not planning to meet Lily Fortune."

"Sure you are. She's hosting a children's picnic Sunday

after next at the ranch. The department is going to be there with the engine we're retiring. Kids love climbing on a fire truck. Even an old one. For obvious reasons, I got roped into being the liaison for the event. You have to have heard about it. The Foundation's the main sponsor."

And she'd answered plenty of questions from people calling the office about its "Fortune February Fest," designed to give underprivileged kids from as far away as Houston a real Texas ranch experience, but that hadn't meant she'd be attending. "I heard they had all the volunteers they needed for the event."

"There's always room for another pair of hands at something like this. Besides. I can't go without a date."

She let out an exasperated sigh. "Nobody takes dates to an event like that."

"How do *you* know?"

Because she'd attended plenty of them with her family. The agreeable, dutiful daughter who'd dressed up and smiled prettily for the society page cameras whenever they'd turned their way. "I just do."

"Come on, Bethany," his voice dropped lower. "You want to make a new life for yourself? Start *living*. Red Rock's a good place."

Why did it affect her so to hear her name on his lips?

She twined the coiled phone cord around her finger. "Are you alone?"

"I'm in my quarters."

Which explained him using her real name.

"Means we're in bed together again," he added. "What are you wearing?"

"Flannel pajamas," she lied repressively and tugged the hem of the departmental blue T-shirt he'd left behind down around her thighs. Almost as quickly as generated electricity had flowed through her house, she'd whipped through her household chores, including the laundry. Tossing his shirt in with her jeans had struck her as an oddly intimate gesture, but she'd had good intentions of returning it to him, folded and ready to wear again.

Of course, that didn't explain why she was now sleeping in it.

"You forget, honey, just how much I like flannel."

She'd forgotten absolutely nothing.

She rolled over and kicked the comforter off her too-warm legs. "The, uh, the field supervisor for the power company finally called me back," she said, deliberately changing the subject. "He said they have to pull a new line from the box. Something like that, anyway. It'll be done by Wednesday, latest."

"Chicken," he murmured.

"That's right," she agreed without a qualm.

She heard him sigh faintly. "What about your car?" he finally asked. "You called your insurance company, right?"

"Yes." And she appreciated the fact that he hadn't tried to take over the matter for her. Instead, he'd merely encouraged her. "They said they'll let me know. They have to determine if the homeowner's insurance is responsible." And she already knew the homeowner's insurance wasn't. "You can get your truck anytime. I figured out a way to get to work." It involved the oldest transportation known to man. Foot.

It would be a couple of miles at least, but walking was good for a pregnant woman. Particularly a woman who'd been used to running every day before fear had sent her running in an entirely different way.

"I'm not in a hurry to get my truck. You can use it from now on as far as I'm concerned."

She pressed her cheek against the pillow. "You have to stop talking like that, Darr."

"Why?"

"Just…because! Because I said so."

He laughed softly, but it was drowned out with a loud, distinct alarm. "Toned out," he said. "That's us. Sweet dreams, Bethany." Once again, he disconnected before she was at all prepared for it and she slowly replaced the receiver.

Sweet dreams, indeed.

When she finally fell back to sleep every one of them seemed to be centered solely on him.

Chapter Nine

"Delivery for—" The teenage kid with a ring in his eyebrow consulted his clipboard. "Barbara Burton?"

Sitting behind the reception desk of the Fortune Foundation, Bethany eyed the enormous vase of brilliant pink and white flowers the boy was holding. She was painfully aware of the attention she was getting from the steady flow of employees moving through the lobby on their way in and out to lunch. "I'm Barbara Burton."

"Cool." The delivery boy set the vase on the desk and flipped the board around to face her. "Sign on line nine, ma'am."

She scrawled Barbara's signature on the line. "Thank you."

"You bet." He grinned. "You're not the only one around town somebody wants to make up with for missing Valentine's Day." He tucked the earphones of his MP3 player in his ear and nearly bounced out the doorway.

"Nice flowers." Julie, one of the teen counselors for the

Foundation, stopped at the desk to pick up the stack of mail that had yet to be sorted. "Better late than never, right?" Her blue eyes twinkled as she headed down the hall.

She hadn't missed Valentine's Day, Bethany thought, running her finger along one of the velvety petals of a spider mum that was as big as a dinner plate.

She'd spent it with Darr.

The phone rang and she automatically hit the button on her headset. "Good afternoon. Thank you for calling the Fortune Foundation. This is Barbara. How may I help you?"

"You look like a woman who needs some lunch."

She sat up straighter in her chair as Darr's deep voice sent shivers down her spine. "Oh? Says who?"

"Me." Darr walked through the doorway, and tucked his cell phone in the pocket of his khaki-colored cargo pants. He rested his wide palms on the reception desk and leaned closer. His blue RRFD shirt tightened over his shoulders. "Nice flowers. Should I be jealous?"

She made a face, though everything inside her was jumping around like water droplets scattered over hot oil. She hadn't seen him since he'd left her house the previous morning.

She'd talked to him.

Dreamt about him.

But she hadn't seen him, and no matter how sternly she'd told herself that what had happened over the weekend had been a result of their enforced proximity, all such common sense flew right out of her mind again when she was face-to-face with him. "You ought to know. You're the one who sent them."

The dimple beside his lips deepened. "So, do the slave drivers around here let you out for good behavior and grub?"

She tucked her tongue between her teeth. He was related in one way or another to a good portion of those supposed slave drivers. "Actually, I took my lunch hour already." And her regret that she'd done so was very real. Peanut-butter-and-cucumber sandwiches were simply nowhere near as appealing as the man leaning against the front of her desk. "I'm sorry."

"Them's the breaks." He pulled his phone out again. "I don't have all that much time, anyway, but I figured I'd give it a shot. Here." He handed her a phone. "I didn't see the truck in the parking lot."

She automatically took the phone, though she held it up curiously. "I…walked to work, actually."

His gaze sharpened on her face. "You walked? What the hell for? There's still snow on the ground for cripes sake and this place is miles from your house!"

And her feet had certainly felt it, particularly by the time she walked the last stretch to reach the three-story building on the highway just outside of town. "It's not too many miles," she countered. "If I were still running every day, this wouldn't even be an issue."

His lips tightened. "You're not running. I left you the keys, for a reason, Be-arbara."

"And I didn't use them for a reason, Darr." She kept her voice low. They were already drawing too much attention.

His jaw was a hard, inflexible line, his dimple nowhere in sight. "Do you get off at five?"

"Four-thirty."

"I'll pick you up then." He spun on his boot heel and headed for the door.

"Darr, wait." She hurriedly unhooked her headset and darted around the desk, chasing after him. "Your phone." She held it out toward him.

He didn't take it, though. "*Your* phone," he said, and pushed out the door before she could argue.

The phone on the desk buzzed, summoning her.

She wanted to ignore it. To chase after the infernal man and make him see reason. Her reason.

But she had a job to do.

Darr would have to wait. She blew out a breath and hurried back to the desk, grabbing up the receiver. "Good afternoon." She launched into her usual spiel. "Thank you for calling the Fortune Foundation…"

"Women," Darr muttered, slamming through the rear entrance to the firehouse. He stomped through the dayroom, which was filled with recliners all facing the enormous flat-screen television hanging on the wall, a pool table and a book-shelf jammed with a mess of books and DVDs.

"They're the opposite sex, son. Would'a hoped you'd learned that by now." Devaney was sprawled back in one of the recliners, an oversize book lying facedown on his chest. His hands were linked behind his curly blond head.

"That book for looks, Vane? We all know you can't read."

Devaney pitched the book at him, but Darr caught it in midair, glancing at the paper cover. A study guide. He flipped the book back at his coworker and turned to the coffee urn that was kept always full and always hot. "You're studying for the exam, eh?"

"Can't let you be the senior LT for long," Devaney said. "'Course you could leave the honors to me if you'd sit for the captain's exam, the way the chief wants you to, instead of being a girl about it."

Until Bethany, Darr hadn't had much interest in going for that promotion, even though the fire chief had practically begged him to. Lately, though, the idea was taking root in the back of his mind.

Lately, since he'd decided to get married.

He filled a mug with the brew, and proceeded to singe the skin off his tongue when he drank it too fast.

"What're you hanging around here for, anyway?" Devaney asked. "You're off today and tomorrow."

"So are you and you're here."

"Yeah, but I ain't got a life," Devaney drawled. He scratched his oft-broken nose. "And you're setting up house with that pretty blond thing over at the Foundation."

"I'm not setting up house."

"Man, I know about that generator you sent over there. And she's driving your precious truck all over town. Sounding pretty cozy to me."

All over town. But not to her job. "Who told you about the truck?"

"Lorena, when she was dishing up my extra-crispy bacon and hash browns. She's the one you were with over the weekend, right?"

"Lorena? Hell, no."

Devaney flipped him off. "The blonde. Lorena says she's the one you pulled outta Red the night of the burn. The one we all know you were trying to track down."

"Lorena's full of information," Darr returned. "She know if the fire investigator's report is in yet on the incident?"

"God, you're touchy," Devaney complained. "Guess you didn't get any after all. Some good lovin' would'a made you a mite friendlier."

Darr shook his head. "You're a sleaze, Vane. Anyone ever tell you that?"

"My mama, every day." Devaney rolled himself off the recliner and stretched. "Report came in this morning," he said with all seriousness. "Definitely arson. Chief went over to Red to talk to the Mendozas about it. I hear the whole clan is working on the place to get it open again. Imagine they'll have their wedding reception there."

"Who?"

"Jorge Mendoza and Jane Gilliam," Devaney said as if it were obvious.

"You know," Darr eyed the other man. "You and Lorena Evans are perfect for each other. You should marry her instead of clogging your arteries with bacon fat every morning at SusieMae's counter. The two of you are like peas in a pod. Whatever she doesn't know about the people in this town, you do."

"It's a filthy job, but somebody's got to do it." Devaney grinned, strolling out of the dayroom.

But not before making a production of setting the study guide next to Darr's elbow.

Ignoring the guide, he dumped the rest of his coffee down the drain and headed out, too.

He'd been on the promotional fast track in LA. Maybe if he'd been less interested in making the next pay grade, he'd have been more interested in keeping Celia safe.

It wasn't far from the firehouse to Red, but behind the wheel of the Double Crown truck he'd purloined from Nick, every second of the way reminded him of Bethany walking to work that morning.

In the short time it took him to get to the restaurant, his jaw ached from grinding his teeth. There was no sign of the fire chief's unit when he parked nearby, so Darr presumed he'd finished delivering the news about the investigation.

Though much of the celebrated hacienda-style restaurant had been damaged by the fire, the worst of the exterior debris had been cleared away within days of the fire investigator's go-ahead. Inside, though, Darr knew that the kitchen—where the burn had started—had been off-limits. Now, with the investigation completed, they'd be able to get started on repairs there, too.

He went in through the courtyard side where snow still clung in the shadows of the walls, looking highly at odds with the tall fan palms that towered overhead. The palms didn't look like they'd suffered too badly from the snowstorm, but the bougainvillea that proliferated around the perimeter of the courtyard was already brown and shriveled.

He knew from experience, though, that the colorful shrubs would recover. They could be cut down to stumps and a month later come back lush and vibrant. In California, every year his mother had carried on a running argument with their gardener to cut back the thorny bushes and every year, had complained when they'd always grown back. He'd always figured she must not have minded them too badly or she simply would have had them dug out at the roots.

In the courtyard of the restaurant, the tables and chairs with their vivid umbrellas overhead, which had been filled with diners the night of the fire, had all been cleared away; and the courtyard would have been bare if not for the old fountain in the center. It was dry for the moment, but Darr figured water would be trickling down its ancient lines soon enough. Assuming none of the plumbing had been damaged by the freezing temperatures they'd just suffered, that is.

Despite the chilliness of the day, the door to the inside restaurant was propped open and he followed the high-pitched whine of an electric saw. As soon as Roberto Mendoza spotted him, the other man straightened where he was leaning over a table saw, and the whine died. "Darr," he greeted, sliding his safety glasses off his face. "Suppose you've heard the news."

"It doesn't change the damage that's been done, but at least your dad has an official stamp on what he's maintained all along."

Roberto pushed a hand through his dark hair, leaving a trail of sawdust behind. "Someone set the fire deliberately." His voice was grim. "There are times when I'm not sure that doesn't feel worse."

That was understandable. The Mendozas were like the Fortunes. You didn't mess with them and expect to get away with it for long. "I figured José would be around here."

"He took my mother home." Roberto's brooding gaze drifted around the walls. Water stains had replaced the historic tapestries that had once hung there.

"How long are you staying before you have to get back to Denver?" Darr knew the other man was in construction and real estate development there.

"As long as it takes." Roberto slid on his safety glasses, clearly intent on resuming his work.

"Well. Tell your folks that if there's anything I can—"

"Do. I know." Roberto's smile was faint, but it was there. "You've done plenty already. You and the rest of the department are why there's something left for us to rebuild." He flipped on the saw and Darr took the cue, heading out with a brief wave.

He intended to take care of a few chores at his apartment before picking up Bethany and taking her home. Convincing her that he should stay with her for the night might be a little tricky, but he intended to do that, too.

But his phone buzzed before he reached the Double Crown truck, and that put paid to everything but heading straight back to the firehouse.

* * *

By the time four-thirty rolled around and her workday was over, Bethany had managed to work her nerves into a fine frenzy anticipating Darr's arrival.

Only it was Nick Fortune who strolled by the reception desk just as she was retrieving her purse from the locked drawer where she kept it. "Darr had to go out on a call," he said. "Multicar pileup halfway between here and San Antone. I'm here to play chauffeur."

"That's not necessary," Bethany said swiftly. Her nervous energy dissipated in a tidal wave of relief. She refused to entertain the idea that it was disappointment sinking through her.

"You have another ride?" Nick had a pair of glasses perched low on his nose, but his brown eyes peered at her over the frames. He was wearing a suit, yet managed to look as relaxed and laid-back as if he were strolling a beach in flip-flops.

And oddly, she couldn't seem to make herself utter the blatant lie that she did have a ride.

What was it about the Fortune men?

"No," she admitted. "But I can walk."

"Yeah. Darr warned me about that. Sugar, it's too damn cold for you to walk all that way." He jangled the car keys in his palm. "Come on. Easier for us both if we go along with the plan. Otherwise, that brother of mine'll drive us both up a tree. He acts like a good ol' boy, but you might have noticed he's pretty much a dog with a bone when he gets something into his head."

Bethany tucked her tongue between her teeth and wondered just how much Nick knew about the "something" that Darr had in his head where she was concerned. "I've noticed." She slid into her coat and accompanied Darr's brother out the door.

She'd expected to find the big white truck that he'd been

driving the previous morning in the parking lot, but instead he led her to a low-slung black Porsche.

Ordinarily, she would have appreciated the lines of the vehicle. But it was nearly identical to the one that Lyle drove.

Nick opened her door and waited until she'd slid down into the passenger seat before closing it and heading around to his side.

"Did he say how bad the accident was?" Bethany asked when they were on the road, heading back through the center of Red Rock.

"Bad enough they called out Red Rock and San Antonio." Nick smoothly navigated around a slower-moving truck and turned into the neighborhood that would lead to Bethany's street. "I don't know how he has the stomach for the stuff he's seen and can still go out every day knowing he might see worse." He pulled to a minimal stop at a stop sign and gave her a sideways glance. "Being married to a firefighter isn't easy under the best of circumstances."

She felt her face go hot. "I guess I don't have to wonder any longer if he told you he'd proposed."

"Darr's a straight shooter." Nick's voice was quiet. "He's strong and he's tough and I respect the hell out of him. And whatever your deal is with Darr, it's your business. I just don't ever want to see him tear himself up again like he did in California after Celia died."

She started. "How did she die?"

He slanted a look her way, looking as if he were debating whether to say anything more.

"How?"

He made a face. "The guy she was living with beat her to death."

Bethany felt nauseated.

"Darr thinks he should have been able to save her."

Bethany curled her fingers around the buttons on her coat. Tears stung her eyes and she stared blindly out the side window. No wonder Nick wasn't praising Darr's marriage proposal. "He's fortunate to have a family who cares." Her voice was thick.

She could feel Nick's gaze on her, but he'd evidently figured he'd said enough as he continued driving out to her house. When he turned up the hill, she could hear the spit of gravel under his tires. Lyle would have had a fit driving his precious car over such a road. "I should have had you let me off at the bottom of the hill. The gravel might damage your—" her voice trailed off at the sight of the unfamiliar black sedan parked in front of her house "—paint job," she finished faintly.

"Looks like you have company." Nick started to turn into her driveway. Snow still lay in the deep ruts, making them easy to spot and avoid, which only seemed to hasten the end of the journey as Nick pulled to a stop near the other vehicle.

"I'm not expecting any." The windows of the sedan were darkened, giving no hint to the identity of who might be sitting inside.

She racked her brain for an excuse, *any* excuse not to get out of the vehicle.

Her palms were sweating and her stomach rose in her throat.

If it were Lyle or some minions sent by her parents to drag her home, she doubted that throwing up all over their shoes would stop them.

"Hey." Nick touched her sleeve. "I really didn't intend to upset you. Are you all right?"

"Actually," she didn't have to fake the trembling in her hand when she pressed it to her abdomen. "I'm suddenly not feeling very well." She ducked her chin when a cramp made her gasp. "Oh, please, not now." But another spasm twisted through her.

"Not now *what?*" Nick was looking vaguely green. "Maybe we should get you inside."

She shook her head. "I'm sorry. Not inside. I—" She gritted her teeth against another wrenching pain. "The hospital," she finally managed. "I think something's wrong with the baby."

Utter silence filled the vehicle for the span of a heartbeat. "I knew it," he muttered under his breath.

Then he wheeled the car right around the other sedan, holding his hand over her shoulder to keep her steady as he rocketed out to the road. "Hold tight," he said. .

There was little else for Bethany to do. The sharp pain was radiating up her spine. Down her legs.

She closed her eyes and tried not to panic but she was pretty much wracked with it when, a short while later, Nick was hustling her through the emergency room, barking for a nurse and nudging her down onto one of the wheelchairs that were sitting near the entrance.

She supposed it was the influence of the Fortune name that garnered such immediate attention, because hardly a minute had passed before she was being whisked through the double doors. One nurse helped her onto the examining table, another was pulling out blood pressure cuffs and a third was wielding a sheaf of forms. "Do you want Mr. Fortune to come back with you, Ms. Burton?"

Another pain clawed at her. "Darr," she managed, breathing hard. "Please can someone call Darr?"

"Where is she?" The emergency room doors were still sliding open when Darr strode inside, spotting Nick, who was leaning his hip against the reception desk, chatting up the starchy gray-haired woman who manned the station.

In Darr's experience, Beatrice was a true battle-ax. God knew that getting any information out of her about Bethany after the fire had been about as pleasant and productive as banging his head with a tire iron.

With Nick, of course, Beatrice was nothing but smiles.

"They ran some tests," Nick said. "I think the doc is with her." He slid off the desk. "I think I need to tell you something before you go back and see her."

"Later."

"But—"

Darr strode past his brother and pushed through the doorway.

If the highway accident he'd just come from had resulted in more injuries instead of deaths, the E.R. would have been busy as hell. As it was, the only survivors had been medevaced to San Antonio and, for now here, there was only one bed with a curtain around it.

When he stepped inside the curtain, his damn knees felt weak.

Bethany was lying on her side on the narrow bed, wearing a washed-out hospital gown with a thin blanket drawn up over her hips. "Hey." His voice was soft.

Her gaze ran over him, taking in the sight of him still in his turnouts. "You came straight from the accident?"

He'd done something he'd never done before. Left a scene early.

He rolled the metal stool close to the bed, straddling it. He closed his hand around hers. "What happened?" All he knew was Nick's version when he'd phoned Darr, and that had been damn abbreviated.

"The baby's fine," she said.

He pressed her fingertips to his lips. Thank God for that. "And you?"

"Why didn't you tell me about Celia?"

He went still. "What about her?"

Her eyes closed. "Your brother told me she died. How she died."

He muttered an oath.

"Don't be angry with him. He's concerned about you."

"He doesn't need to be. It was a long time ago and has nothing to do with us."

She didn't look entirely convinced.

"It doesn't." He slid his fingers through the ends of her waving hair. "I'm concerned about *you*. Here. Now. What did the doctor say?"

Her eyes looked like bruises above her pale cheeks. "Dr. Waite thinks I had an anxiety attack."

Anxiety they could deal with. "About what Nick told you, or about the car parked at your house?"

She moistened her lips. "He told you about it, I suppose."

"Yes." It was one thing Darr didn't want to throttle him over.

"He thinks you've lost your mind where I'm concerned."

"Nick can think whatever he wants," he said quietly. "As tight as we are, we live our own lives our own way. He's no different. This—" he wagged his finger between himself and her "—is between us. You and me. *That's* what I care about."

The tip of her nose got pinker. Her eyes glistened. "I don't think I've had anyone care…really care…in a long time." Her lips quivered and she pressed them together, clearly struggling. "Maybe ever," she finally added.

"You have someone now." He folded his arm on the narrow strip of bed beside the thin pillow beneath her head. He rested his chin on his arm. Mere inches separated them. "Who did you think was in the car?" He figured he already knew.

"Lyle." Her lips turned down at the corners.

Now the slug he wanted to pound into the ground had a name.

"It was your landlord," Darr told her softly.

Her eyes widened. She struggled to sit up, and the hospital gown slid off one shoulder. "How do you know that? The owners live in San Antonio."

He sat up, too. "After Nick called me, I asked a friend at the PD to check it out. The guy was still there, meeting some contractor to fix the carport."

She slid the gown back over her shoulder, but since the tie behind her neck had obviously come loose, it just slipped back down again. "Just the owner." She pressed her palm over her eyes. "I can't believe I was such a ninny."

"Panic doesn't have anything to do with being a ninny," he dismissed. But it was one more indication of the terror that had forced her to assume a false identity. "You're one of the bravest young women I've ever met."

Her hand slowly dropped. "How can you say that?"

"For one thing, you're not running back to the guy who hurt you." *Lyle.* He couldn't bring himself to voice the man's name, though. "You'd be surprised at the number of women who do. The women who believe the jerks when they claim to be sorry, or that they'll never do it again."

"Is that what Celia did?"

He nodded.

Her brow wrinkled. "I stayed with him even after he hit me."

"But you *did* leave. You haven't gone back. You're making a life the best way you know how. You're standing on your own two feet, honey. That's not ninny. That's brave."

She was looking at him as if she badly wanted to believe him. "Do you—"

"Okay, Ms. Burton." The statement came from the young doctor in a lab coat who shoved aside the curtain more fully with the metal clipboard he held to make room for the even younger-looking boy wheeling a mobile ultrasound unit. "Hello, Darr."

"What's going on?" Darr eyed the equipment.

"We're doing an ultrasound."

"Thought it was an anxiety attack."

"It's just a precaution," the doctor assured. The technician ignored them all as he rolled the unit closer to the bed.

"Heard they sent two patients over to the trauma center in San Antonio from that pileup." The doctor nodded toward him, taking in Darr's appearance. "You work it?"

"Yeah." He was more interested in getting the ultrasound going than rehashing the grisly scene.

The doctor had turned to set his medical chart on the short counter and was pumping antiseptic wash onto his hands. "Three of the vics were kids?" He rinsed away the wash.

"Good Lord," Bethany said, obviously horrified.

"How long before she can go home?" Darr deliberately changed the subject.

The doctor dried his hands and pitched the paper towel through the hole in the counter designed for waste. "Soon as we see how the baby is doing." He smiled at Bethany and took the rolling stool that Darr had vacated.

Evidently satisfied with the position of his equipment, the technician adjusted the head of Bethany's bed, and she lay back down. He adjusted her gown and squirted gel on her bare belly, then handed the doctor the transducer.

"All rightie. Let's see how things are going." Dr. Waite pressed the scanner against Bethany's abdomen, sliding it through the gel as he stared at the monitor. "You said this is your first ultrasound?"

"Mmm-hmm."

Darr moved to the other side of Bethany's bed. She, too, was staring at the monitor, her lower lip caught between her teeth.

He closed his hand over hers.

She didn't pull away.

"There's the baby." Dr. Waite circled his finger in front of the monitor. "Placenta looks good. Position looks good." He glanced at Bethany. Noted their linked hands and his gaze almost imperceptibly shifted to include Darr. "Do you want to know the sex?"

Bethany's gaze flitted up to meet Darr's.

Something squeezed hard inside him. "Time to decide." His voice was husky. He cleared his throat. "It's absolutely your choice."

The corner of Bethany's lips curved. She looked back at the doctor. "Yes."

Dr. Waite looked at the monitor; slid the scanner around a little more. "Looks like your son isn't all that shy," he said, smiling. "*Definitely* a boy." He leaned forward and grabbed the medical chart. "We'll send the results over to your OB in San Antonio, but from what I can see, all looks well." His pen scratched on the chart. "I'll send the nurse in to do another blood pressure check, and if you're still in the normal range, we'll get you out of here and back home." He glanced up. "Any questions?"

"No. Thank you, Dr. Waite." Bethany was still staring at the image on the monitor.

Darr sort of knew how she felt.

He could hardly tear his gaze away, either, and barely noticed when the doctor left.

"We'll print that for you," the technician said with an understanding look as he shut down the equipment. "You'll have it before you leave," he said and pushed the cart beyond the curtain that he drew back around the area.

Bethany's fingers were still twined with Darr's.

He had to swallow the knot that was still in his throat. "There's just one thing left for you to do now," he told her. "Start thinking of names for your son."

"Darr," she whispered quietly.

"What?"

She shook her head slightly. "No. I mean as a name."

She refused to marry him—so far—but she would consider naming her child after him?

It was a good thing the curtain was being drawn back again by a nurse, who pulled down the blood pressure cuff from where it was hanging near the bed.

"Don't torture the kid that way," Darr managed lightly, moving out of the way so the nurse could slide the cuff around Bethany's arm. "Believe me. Growing up with the name Darwin ain't easy."

She was silent as the nurse worked the blood pressure monitor. But as soon as the nurse finished and departed again after telling Bethany she could get dressed, she spoke.

"I'd like to think he would grow up to be as good and decent as you."

Darr sat on the bed beside her. "Then say you'll marry me."

Her eyes were wide. Color suffused her high cheekbones. "Darr—" She was shaking her head slightly.

He slid his hand along her cheek, stilling the motion. "Just say you'll think about it. *Really* consider it."

She moistened her lips. Blinked. "Okay," she finally said. "I'll consider it."

He exhaled and tipped her head and pressed his lips to her forehead. Pressing her for more could wait.

"Will you get me out of here?"

"I'll have you under your roof as soon as you're dressed."

"*Your* roof. I'd rather go home with you."

He pulled back, and though her purple-blue gaze was shy, it was unswerving. "If that's all right."

"Yeah," he managed. "That's definitely all right."

Chapter Ten

"It's not large or fancy," Darr said, as he conducted the brief tour of his apartment when they arrived. "But it's enough for me. For now," he added pointedly.

The place was easily twice the size of her rented house.

Primarily because he had a bedroom.

Bethany stood in the doorway of said room and eyed the bed—covered in a thoroughly bachelorlike blue plaid comforter—that consumed a healthy portion of the space.

"It's very nice," she assured him. Clean, and possessing a sort of emptiness that wasn't uncomfortable, but more an echo of the limited time he'd said he spent there.

He waved his hand over a dresser drawer he pulled open. "T-shirts. Sweats. Use whatever you need." Then he walked out of the bedroom. "Bathroom's there," he pointed at the opened doorway adjacent to the bedroom. "I'm sorry that I've got to leave you again."

She shook her head. Once they'd left the hospital, he'd warned her that he'd have to go back to the firehouse. "I understand. It's your job." The man was still wearing his turnout pants, for pity's sake. The heavy khaki-colored pants with orange fluorescent stripes around the bottom were unfastened at the waist, hanging over his dark blue T-shirt-clad shoulders by red suspenders.

He looked the part of the ultimate hero.

He could say that she wasn't a ninny, but what else explained her hiding out now at *his* place because she was too frightened to go back to her own?

She brushed down the sleeves of her sweater.

"Are you cold?" He immediately reached for the thermostat on the wall in the hallway.

"I'm fine," she insisted. "Go." She swished her hands toward the door. He'd already spent a good portion of the dwindling evening on her.

"I hate leaving you."

"I'll be fine."

"I know that," he said easily. "I just want to enjoy the sight of you here."

Warmth spread through her face.

And the rest of her.

His eyes crinkled then, almost as if he were perfectly aware of her reaction. And maybe he was.

"I'll be back before you have to go to work. I'll run you back to your place for clothes, get my truck, and you'll still be sitting at your desk on time tomorrow."

She nodded. He'd already gone through the logistics with her.

"There's plenty of food in the fridge," he added as he opened the door. "Make sure you feed that boy of yours. He's probably starving by now." With a flash of that deadly dimple beside his crooked grin, he pulled the door closed after him.

She exhaled and pressed her hand against the faint, rhythmic flutter she could feel.

Her boy.

She blew out a breath and looked out the large window over his kitchen sink. Though it was well past dark, she could see the street outside easily, courtesy of the tall lamppost casting its golden glow, not only over the street, but over the cluster of lacy-leafed bushes around its base. Snow was still piled over the curbs where the snowplows had pushed it, piled over the manicured strip of lawn that stretched between the sidewalk and the curb.

The white truck Darr was using had already driven out of sight.

She nibbled her lip and turned to the refrigerator. In comparison to her ancient one, the tall stainless steel model of Darr's was nearly space-age. And as he'd said, it had plenty inside. She was vaguely surprised that the contents were similar to what had been in hers before the snow hit.

Except he had a six-pack of some oddly named beer that she'd never heard of.

She poured herself a glass of milk, made a turkey sandwich and turned on the television.

His had a spectacularly clear picture, of course.

She found the nightly news, turned down the volume and gave up trying to curtail her curiosity. The dark wood bookcase against one wall contained an eclectic collection—from baseball caps to books on philosophy.

There was one shelf with several haphazardly arranged framed photographs. She picked up the largest frame—a beautifully matted eight-by-ten that obviously dated back many years. It was easy to pick out Darr. Not only did he look the youngest, sprawled on the floor in front of his seated parents, but she would recognize that crooked grin and dimple anywhere. She could even pick out Nick. He was the one wearing a violently hued, tie-dyed T-shirt. He, and the other three boys—blond-haired to brown—were standing around the adults.

And even though they had all posed, remaining still long enough for the person behind the camera to snap the shot, there was life and energy screaming from the photograph. Energy that was singularly lacking in any sort of formal studio shot. At least when it came to the chronicles of *her* family that her mother had insisted upon so that she could hang them in her father's office.

Testament to their quote-un-quote perfect family.

She drew the tip of her fingernail along the glass.

The Fortunes looked happy. The kind of happy that far transcended fortune.

She set the frame back on the shelf and peered at the rest of the photographs. Christmases. A birthday—someone's twenty-first, if the drunken pink elephant on the cake top and the laughing crowd of guests surrounding it with beer bottles held aloft were any indication.

For her twenty-first birthday, her father had introduced her to Lyle for the first time during a cocktail party thrown, not to celebrate her birthday, but to court another infusion of cash into the family coffers. At twenty-one, Bethany had been thoroughly uninterested in the family business. Maybe if she'd paid more attention, she would have realized sooner the part she was unwittingly playing in the arrangement between her father and Lyle. Instead, after a year of continual nagging from her mother about what a good catch Lyle made, she'd agreed to accompany him to the Governor's Ball. To her surprise, he'd been an enjoyable companion. Humorous and certainly handsome. And even though he could have had his pick of any number of females, he'd continued to pursue her. He hadn't even been swayed by her resistance to sleeping with him.

If anything, the longer she put him off, the more concerted his courtship became.

Of course, the more she saw of Lyle, the better her parents liked it. When she'd accompanied Lyle to Switzerland on a ski trip, she'd known that she'd end up sharing his bed. There hadn't been any bottle rockets going off inside her afterward, but that hadn't stopped him from proposing. Or her from accepting.

Everything about that was wrong. So wrong. Even if he had never lifted his hand against her, it had been wrong.

A trilling ring startled her out of her thoughts and it took her a moment to realize that it was the cell phone that Darr had given her that was ringing. By the time she'd fumbled it out of her purse, it had stopped.

She slid it open and scrolled through the numbers that he'd stored in the phone's memory.

Darr's home. Darr's work. Darr's cell phone.

She dialed his cell.

He picked up immediately. "You settling in all right?"

She felt a foolish smile on her lips and hugged the sudden warmth sliding through her close. "You haven't even been gone an hour."

"Feels longer. What're you doing?"

"Eating a sandwich." It was close to the truth. She'd taken a few bites before getting sidetracked by the photographs. "What're you doing?"

"Putting together giveaway bags for the kids next weekend. Gotta work on 'em when we can."

She sank farther into the corner of his very comfortable couch and nibbled off a corner of bread from her sandwich. "Red Rock's not *that* large. How many calls do you have?"

"Oh, you'd be surprised. Structure fires are actually the smallest percentage. The fire at Red was the worst we've seen in a while."

"I don't suppose it's easy to catch an arsonist." He'd told her the fire had been deliberately set.

"Not always. But Red Rock is a tight community. If the guy is still around, he'll make a slip sooner or later. You're not having nightmares or anything, are you? About the fire?"

"No." Amazingly, she wasn't. Her nightmares were of an entirely different sort. "Quite honestly, I hardly remember anything from that night." Except him.

Her gaze fell on the well-coiffed newscaster looking out from the television screen, his expression sober while above his shoulder rolled footage of several mangled vehicles. "You probably see more car accidents than fires, then."

"Yeah. Not too many like the pileup on the highway today, though."

"It's on the news right now." She reached for the remote and turned it off. "Watching *that* is bad enough. How do you stand it?"

"Focus on the ones who live. Some days that's harder than others. It's bad when there are kids involved. It was pretty grim."

She slid a little farther down into the couch. "I hope you haven't had to see anything worse."

"I wish I hadn't."

Which meant that he had.

"Tell me what's in the giveaway bags," she said suddenly. "Don't want to think anymore about tragedies for tonight?"

"I don't want *you* to think about it," she said softly.

He was silent for a moment. "Whistles," he finally said, his voice low. "Fire safety coloring books."

"Anything else?"

"Snack bars donated by SusieMae's. Crayons donated by the Mendozas. And 'course we'll have the old engine there with a few of the guys who work my shift."

"What about Nick?"

He exhaled. "Even if I weren't pissed at him, he wouldn't be there. It's a kids' event and he doesn't do kids."

"You shouldn't be angry with him."

"He upset you. That's always going to make me angry—" A high-pitched alarm nearly drowned out his voice. "That's our tone," he said more loudly. Behind him, she could hear a female voice calling out numbers. "You can hear why we work on stuff when we can."

"Be careful," she said quickly.

"Honey, I'm always careful," he returned.

And just that quickly, the line went dead.

She exhaled, pressing her hand to her bumping heart. Whether it was adrenaline because of the alarm or because of Darr, she wasn't entirely certain. She had a strong suspicion, though, that it was the latter.

She finished her sandwich, tidied up the kitchen, and still feeling very much out of her depth, entered his bedroom.

The dresser drawer he'd left open beckoned and, trying not to be too distracted by the bed, she gingerly poked through the neat contents, pulling out a gray long-sleeved T-shirt and a pair of sweatpants. They'd be way too big, but the drawstring waist could be tightened, and the elastic cuffs could be folded up.

If Darr's apartment was twice the size of her house, his

bathroom was also more than double the size of hers. For one thing, he didn't have a stacked washer/dryer unit taking up one corner.

For another, not only did he have an enormous, oval-shaped garden tub, but he had a separate glass-walled shower enclosure, as well.

She hardly debated the matter.

She flipped on the water in the tub, adjusting it so that it was comfortably warm but not hot. No bath salts, of course, but that didn't matter. Just being able to stretch out in a luxuriously sized tub was enough to make her feel nearly giddy.

She didn't get out until the water was cold and she was in danger of falling asleep right there in his tub. She let out the water, then felt thoroughly extravagant by stepping into the shower and washing her hair there, before wrapping herself in one of the oversize blue towels folded on the shelf. With the comb from her purse, she worked out the tangles from her hair.

Despite looking for one, she couldn't find a blow-dryer, and she had to settle for towel-drying her hair as best she could. She'd just have to suffer the ringlet results of her shower greed.

The sweatpants were as oversize as she'd expected. The waist, however, didn't need tightening quite as much as she'd thought it would. A fact that led her to stand on tiptoe in front of the wide mirror atop Darr's bedroom dresser, studying the profile of her growing belly.

Then her gaze shifted, taking in the entire picture of herself.

Instead of the petite, sleek-haired, pampered-looking debutante she'd been, she saw a wide-eyed, tangle-haired woman.

The woman that Darr, amazingly, seemed to want.

She dropped the long T-shirt over her thickening waist and faced the bed.

Two choices.

Climb under the comforter covering that mile-wide bed, or snitch a pillow and sleep on his couch. It was certainly more comfortable than hers was—whether it was pulled out into a bed or not. And Darr hadn't made any suggestion, one way or another where she should sleep when she'd invited herself into his home.

When she'd been with Lyle, he'd made it plain that he was the one who called the shots. He was the initiator. The decision maker. And—as he'd proven when she'd become pregnant—he didn't have much tolerance when situations arose without his say-so.

If she'd ever stripped off her nightgown and invited him boldly into her bed, he'd have been thoroughly disapproving.

Darr had *not* disapproved.

She threw off her indecision and tossed back a corner of the comforter, climbing into the side of the bed away from the digital clock sitting on the nightstand.

Darr was not Lyle. And she was not a ninny.

Feeling better than she had in weeks, she was asleep almost as soon as her head hit the pillow and miraculously didn't waken until she felt the bed dip. "Darr?"

"Shh. Go back to sleep."

She peered into the soft dark night. "I thought you wouldn't be back until morning." It clearly wasn't morning.

His arm slid around her waist. "I got off a few hours early. I wanted to see if there was a snow angel really sleeping in my bed." His voice whispered over the back of her neck.

She melted.

There simply was no other word for it.

"I'm glad." She slid her hand along his arm. His warm, bare arm. Her fingers slid over the back of his hand, sliding between his. "I like it here."

"Told you my bed was comfortable."

She smiled into the darkness. "The bed's not the reason I like it."

"That works for me, too." He brushed her hair away from her cheek and kissed her jaw.

She twisted her head around and found his mouth with hers.

"Keep doing that," he murmured eventually, "and neither one of us is going to be sleeping any time soon."

"That works for me," she whispered in return. She drew their linked hands to her breast.

He let out a low breath. Through the soft knit of his shirt, his thumb rubbed across her tight nipple, making it rise even more achingly. "You need your sleep."

"I need you." She wriggled around, turning to face him. "I shouldn't, but I do."

"Need isn't a bad thing." Beneath the blanket, his hand snuck beneath the hem of her T-shirt. There was nothing but bare skin beneath.

Her voice went thready as she sucked in air at the wicked glide. "It can be bad," she managed breathlessly.

"Yes. But not now. Not this."

He grazed his fingertips over her hip. Down her thigh, drawing it over his and his mouth caught hers and he kissed her so tenderly, so thoroughly, that she forgot the cautions that wanted to lurk inside her head. And when he slipped, so smoothly, so completely into her, and her name was a rough exhale on his lips, something inside her cracked open wide.

Even though she wanted to savor him, hover endlessly in that sweet, sweet fullness, her body quickened.

She could feel his heartbeat as if it were her own. Shared the slow, deepening breaths he drew. Impossibly felt him even deeper, even fuller.

As if he were breaching her heart.

Her soul.

Tremors quaked. Built strength. Speed. She gasped his name, and his arms held her even closer. His breath burned against her ear. "Let it go."

It was too late, though. She was already spinning into the universe. And even dissolving into splintering pleasure, she could feel his, too, just as keenly, and it drove her even higher. Harder.

Tears collected behind her closed lids. Streamed down her temples. And always, always, his arms held her close as they tumbled into that beckoning, timeless abyss.

An eternity seemed to pass before the world found motion again.

She pulled in a long breath. Let it out again.

He thumbed away the tears sliding silently down her cheek. "Did I hurt you?"

She felt healed, in ways that she couldn't even begin to explain, not even to herself. "You didn't hurt me."

"Then why the tears?"

"Too much perfection," she whispered. "Thank you."

He let out a breath that seemed to come from deep, deep inside him. "Thank you."

"For what?"

"Being here to come home to." His head slowly fell to her shoulder.

A fresh wave of emotion burned the back of her eyes.

She brushed her fingers through his thick hair. Wordlessly pressed her lips to his brow.

Neither one of them moved as sleep claimed them.

Her car was still a pancake of metal, covered in wood debris, when Darr drove her to her house the next morning before work.

Nearly all the snow had melted away in the yard, leaving the ruts in her driveway looking even worse than they had before the storm.

"It's a pathetic sight," she said as he pulled his borrowed Double Crown truck to a stop behind his own black pickup. "Imagine you've seen worse, though."

"Yup." He climbed out of the truck and came around to open her door, then continued to hold her arm, even when she was on the ground. "Careful. The mud is slick."

They made it up the steps and she unlocked the door. "It'll only take me a few minutes to dress." She'd barely stepped out of the quick shower she'd taken that morning at his place when he'd popped a piece of thick, sourdough toast into her mouth. That had been followed up by amazingly delectable scrambled eggs.

She'd accused him of hiding his cooking prowess.

He'd drawled that food tasted better after a night like they'd just shared.

She'd blushed.

Until meeting him, she'd never *had* nights like that.

"You have plenty of time before you need to be at the office," he assured her now. "Pack that fancy suitcase of yours as full as it can get. We'll come get the rest of your stuff later."

He seemed to take it for granted that she'd be staying with him now.

She nibbled the inside of her lip and didn't challenge the assumption.

After all, isn't that what she wanted?

When she was with him she felt safe. Home.

So, after pulling on a slim pair of black slacks and a tailored pink shirt with shirttails long enough to cover the unfastened waistband of her slacks, she did as he suggested.

Most of the clothing she'd acquired in the last few months fit into the suitcase. She even added her toiletries, vitamins and herbal teas and there was still room to spare.

She opened the bottom drawer of the dresser and pulled out her grandmother's pearls.

The last time she'd worn them had been with the wedding gown.

Now she coiled them several times around her neck and they still looped down across her chest. Without a second thought, she nudged the drawer closed again, leaving the fancy peignoir sets behind.

Then she slid her secondhand peacoat onto her shoulders, pulled up the handle of her suitcase, and rolled it out to the porch, locking the door behind her.

Darr, wearing blue jeans and an unbuttoned plaid flannel shirt over a white T-shirt, looked up at her. He propped his hands on his hips and shook his head.

She pressed her hand against her chest, looking down at herself, but couldn't see anything amiss. "What?"

"Sometimes I can't get over it. How damn beautiful you are."

She felt herself flush. She'd grown up wearing designer labels. Now the only thing of value she wore were the pearls.

"It shows, you know," he added. "You look—"

"—fat?"

"Yeah, right. Pregnant. Definitely pregnant. You're ready to announce it to everyone who sees you today?"

She hadn't thought about it, really, until she'd exchanged his sweatpants and T-shirt for her own clothing. "Yes. And everyone who sees me tomorrow. And the next day, and the next."

His eyes were nearly the same color as the early morning sky and they crinkled. He bounded up the steps and took the suitcase by the handle, easily hefting its weight. "Good for you."

After he'd dumped the suitcase in the back of the white truck, he handed her the keys to his truck, which he'd retrieved from her kitchen counter. "This time you'll drive to the office?"

In hindsight, her refusal to use his truck to get to work seemed silly. She took the keys. "Yes. Thank you. What are you going to do?"

"Catch up on a few Zs," he said, chuckling when the heat rose again in her face. "Return this rig here to Lily's place. I'll get Devaney to follow me out there. We need to go over some planning for the picnic anyway."

Lily's place, she knew, meant the Double Crown. "Okay." She moistened her lips, suddenly feeling awkward.

His lips tilted. He hooked his hand gently behind her neck and drew her close for a slow, sweet kiss.

When he stepped back and pulled open the driver's door to his big truck, she feared her face was even rosier.

Amazingly, she didn't care.

"See you after work," he said, helping her up behind the wheel.

"See you after work," she echoed.

"Gotta drive to the office first, honey," he prompted softly. Amused.

She blinked. Realized the key was still in her hand. She fit it into the ignition and looked over at him warningly. "Don't let this go to your head."

His smile just widened.

And she knew she was never going to be the same.

Chapter Eleven

"I know I've said it about ten times today already, but this has been the most perfect day for a picnic." Lorena Evans stared up at the perfection of the cloudless, blue sky. "Hard to believe that two weeks ago everything in sight was covered in snow. And now—" She broke off, looking around them.

Not a speck of snow remained from the storm to dot the wide expanse of rolling hills and grazing land of the Double Crown. The day held only lengthening golden sunlight that counteracted the steady breeze. It had been neither too cool nor too hot.

The result? Perfect.

All around, the children who'd arrived by the busload earlier in the afternoon, continued racing from one activity to another. Even now, after having watched for several hours, Bethany was hard-pressed to determine what held more appeal for the youngsters.

The long, shining, red fire engine that was parked about a hundred yards away, midway between the banquet tables laden with food and games that the adults were tending and the main ranch house that was surrounded by a sandstone wall, or the weathered barn behind them with its tall, wide doors, thrown open to the treasures within.

It was even a toss-up to determine who was enjoying themselves more.

The adults—who not only included about a dozen volunteers from the Foundation, but a good portion of Red Rock business proprietors, and, of course, their hostess, Lily Fortune, who was every bit as beautiful and gracious as Darr had claimed—or the kids, ranging from wide-eyed kindergartners to middle-schoolers who'd rapidly lost their blasé mien the second Darr and his coworkers rolled up in the behemoth fire engine with all its lights flashing.

The department might be retiring the vehicle, having replaced it with a far more modern rig, but as far as she could tell, it didn't look all that outdated to her.

"It's an amazing sight," Bethany agreed, watching the engine as she absently filled a red plastic cup with apple juice and handed it to the little girl across the table from her. Darr and the guys who'd delivered the generator to her house after the storm all stood alongside the engine, monitoring the half-dozen kids clambering up and down through the opened doors.

"Thanks, Miz Burton," the gap-toothed girl lisped and ran off, carefully balancing her drink cup.

Lorena, working the refreshments beside her that had been provided by SusieMae's, laughed. "Barb, sweetie, you haven't looked at much of anything aside from Darr Fortune's very fine hiney since we started working here this afternoon."

Bethany felt her face flush.

"Can't say I blame you, though," Lorena added. "All those fireboys look pretty darn fine."

Devaney—Bethany still didn't know if that was his first or his last name, despite the evening of pizza he'd shared with her and Darr earlier that week—strolled to their table. He was almost skinny in comparison to Darr's broad shoulders, and his curly white-blond hair looked as if he'd dipped his head too long in a bucket of bleach, but there was something distinctly similar about the two men.

Firefighters, Bethany had rapidly learned in the two weeks since she'd essentially moved in with Darr, all seemed to possess a certain demeanor that set them apart from the rest.

"Hey, there, Barbie doll," Devaney greeted Bethany with a wide grin, though she noticed that his gaze didn't really veer away from the statuesque redhead working beside her. "Fill 'er up, would you please?"

"You got a leak out of those boots of yours, Devaney?" Lorena's voice was sweet. "You've drunk enough juice today to float a boat."

"And I'm smart enough to ask this sweetheart for a refill than to expect you to show some generosity."

Lorena made a face at him and turned to flip open one of the coolers behind them filled with ice and gallon-sized juice and water containers.

Bethany poured the last of her pitcher of apple juice into Devaney's cup, filling it nearly to the brim. "There you go."

"Thank you, darlin'." He winked and strolled back toward the engine.

"Insufferable jerk," Lorena muttered, turning back to the table. She flipped open a water jug and began refilling some of the empty pitchers on the table. "Be grateful for the one you got, sweetie. Wouldn't have thought it, but Darr's definitely the keeper sort."

"Devaney isn't?"

Lorena snorted. "The man doesn't know what the C-word means. Commitment? Please." She dropped the empty jug in the trash barrel beside the table and seemed to toss away the topic of Devaney at the same time. "So, when's that baby bump of yours due to pop?"

Bethany ran her hand over her abdomen. The bright red turtleneck that she wore didn't do a thing to hide her expanding size. To her obstetrician's delight, she'd even been up by four pounds at the appointment that Darr had insisted on accompanying her to last week. "Middle of June."

"You and Darr ever need a babysitter for that tot of yours, you let me know," Lorena said. Her expression was wry. "Seems that taking care of other people's babies is about as close as I'm going to get."

She, like nearly everyone else who'd learned that Bethany was pregnant, didn't seem to question the couple that Darr and Bethany had suddenly become, or the place that her baby would hold in their lives.

Bethany, however, still held onto her doubts.

Everything between her and Darr just seemed too perfect. Too quick. Too easy.

It wasn't that she doubted Darr. Far from it.

It was herself she couldn't quite trust.

Which was why she continued to put him off every morning when he'd ask, "Can I call the preacher now?"

She tore her gaze from Darr's unquestionably fine rear and looked at Lorena. "I guess you want children?"

"Have for as long as I can remember." Lorena rolled her eyes, shaking her head. "Which, at my age, is saying something since I'm not exactly getting any younger. And prospects in Red Rock aren't exactly expanding." Her gaze strayed back toward the fire engine.

Right then and there, Bethany decided that the next time Devaney came for pizza, she'd find some way to include Lorena.

The irony that she didn't doubt there would be a next time wasn't lost on her.

"How are you ladies doing?" Lily Fortune stopped next to them. A wide-brimmed hat shaded her strikingly beautiful face, which age hadn't even begun to dim. "Do you have everything you need? Did you take a break to eat some dinner?"

"Yes. We're fine, Mrs. Fortune," Bethany assured. The woman was about her mother's age—early sixties—but any similarity ended there. Angela Burdett's hair was as falsely blond as Lily Fortune's hair was still naturally dark. Her mother's face stayed smooth courtesy of cosmetic surgery and copious amounts of Botox, while the faint lines radiating from Lily's dark, thickly lashed eyes only seemed to underscore her exotic beauty. "Everyone's having a wonderful time."

"Yes, they are." Lily looked around with a satisfied expression. "My husband is probably looking down on all this with immense pleasure." She gave Bethany a sidelong glance. "You be sure to sit when you have a chance, my dear, or Darr will have both our heads. Oh, there's Emmett and Linda driving up. They've brought the ice cream. Excuse me, won't you?" Her long legs made short work of the distance between the barn and the graded road beyond the fire engine.

Since there seemed to be a lull in the run on beverages, Bethany did sit. Right on top of one of the large white ice chests lined up behind them. "Did you ever meet Mr. Fortune?"

Lorena sat, too, stretching her jean-clad legs in front of her. "Sure. He was a good guy. Handsome as the day is long."

Lorena tsked. "That's one thing you can say about all the Fortunes. They're a good-looking bunch. The whole town grieved when he died." She wrinkled her nose in thought. "Four years now, I'd say. Expect it'd be hard to move on after loving—and losing—a man like that. Oh, sit. Sit." She waved her hand at Bethany and hopped up when a group of giggling teenaged girls approached.

Since it did feel good to get off her feet, Bethany stayed where she was. She stretched out her legs and wriggled her toes inside her tennis shoes. Her gaze roamed over the crowd and she laughed softly when a half-pint of a pigtailed girl whooped and hollered as she beat her opponents in successfully saddling a padded sawhorse with a stuffed horse head attached to one end, and a blue yarn tail attached to the other.

"Nobody's watching." Darr's soft voice suddenly came to her from behind. "We could find an empty stall, spread out some straw—"

She caught his hand as it slipped around her waist. "You're incorrigible."

He laughed and kissed the side of her neck. "It's your fault." He straightened. "Hey, Lorena. How's it going?"

The redhead rolled her eyes, but her smile was indulgent. "Get a room, why don't you?"

"I'm trying," Darr drawled, giving Bethany a devilish wink just for the sheer pleasure of seeing her cheeks go pink. "Come on." He took her hands and drew her to her feet. "I'm a honcho today and I'm calling a fifteen-minute break."

"Can't do much in fifteen minutes," Lorena inserted with a laugh.

Bethany's bright gaze collided with his and he felt that same emotion clamp around his heart that had only been getting stronger since the first time he'd looked into them and had seen forever. "That's what *she* thinks," he murmured for her ears alone.

She muffled a laugh against her fist and followed him into the cool, dim barn where the strong scent of horseflesh and the hay bales stacked high in a puzzlelike maze drew them into its heady hold.

Mercifully, he didn't have to look for a private corner. For the moment, the place was devoid of kids.

It was just him. Her.

And seven curious horses watching them with their liquid brown eyes from the two rows of stalls at the far side of the barn as Darr led her around the side of the mammoth hay maze toward them.

"You're not really looking for an empty horse stall, are you?"

He stopped and leaned back against a wooden rail, next to a spectacular dark bay who tucked his head over Darr's shoulder, looking for his usual treat. "Sorry, fella." He reached up and rubbed the horse's forehead. "No apple for you this time."

Bethany propped her foot on the bottom rail and reached her hand over the top, stroking the horse's black mane. "Hey, sweetheart," she crooned. "Aren't you a handsome one?"

"Barnabus," Darr supplied. "Barney for short." He pointed out the stalls on the facing row. "Double Jeopardy's the roan on this end. Pasqual, Senator Sam, Honeygirl and Mojito's the palomino filly on the far side. It's an apt name. If you don't watch that one close, she'll knock you on your butt." The rest of the horses were outside, turned out in the various corrals.

Bethany rested her cheek on her arm, looking at him. "Do you ride?"

"Occasionally. You?"

She looked back at Barney. Stroked his neck. "I used to ride almost as regularly as I ran. That's what refined young women did in our circle. We were members of the riding club, the yacht club, the junior women's league. The ones who did lunch."

"Do you miss it?"

She shook her head, then paused. "Well. Maybe the riding."

"We'll come back here after the baby's come and you can ride to your heart's content. Lily's always concerned about the horses getting enough attention."

"I like her."

"Most folks do." But he hadn't drawn her away from the crowd for idle chatter. Even now he could smell someone smoking a cigarette nearby, a reminder that they could be interrupted at any moment. But he'd been watching her all day long while he took care of his business and she took care of about a hundred thirsty kids.

And he knew he couldn't wait a minute longer.

"I put in for the next advancement exam," he said abruptly. "Captain. If I pass—" and he knew he would "—and if I get the slot—" also a given, since the chief had told him so "—it'll mean a nice little bump in pay."

Her eyes narrowed slightly. "You don't sound very enthusiastic. Is that what you want?"

"What I want—" he pulled out the small box that had been burning a hole in his pocket since retrieving it from his safe-deposit box days earlier "—is for you to marry me." He thumbed back the lid. "Maybe this will show you how serious I am."

Her eyes widened as her gaze fell on the ring. Her lips parted, but no sound escaped.

The fact that she wasn't already telling him no, or that she was still thinking about it, gave him hope.

"It was my grandmother's. She gave it to me before she died," he added. "She had blue eyes, like yours. My grandfather said the stones reminded him of the color of her eyes." There were five of them, decorating the narrow width of the white gold band, surrounding a center diamond. "I don't even know what the stones are. But she loved the ring and he loved her."

She swallowed. Her eyes had gone wet. "It's beautiful," she whispered. "But Darr—" She broke off. Touched the tip of her tongue to the center of her upper lip. "You, um, you should give this to someone you…you love."

His throat tightened. His nose prickled. He'd never considered giving it to anyone before. Not even Celia. "I am."

Her lashes lifted again. "What?"

He held her gaze. "I think I fell in love with you the first time you opened your eyes and looked at me outside of Red. And then the snowstorm hit when I'd finally found you. Hell, I don't know. Maybe God was taking pity on me so you wouldn't shut the door in my face."

"Oh, Darr."

He could walk into a burning building without a qualm, but he couldn't keep his hand steady when he slid the ring out of the box and held it between them. "I know everything up to now has seemed like one big rush. But we have the rest of our lives together to take our time. This isn't about me doing the rescue thing, though I'd lay down my life to keep you and that baby safe. *Wear my ring.* Be my wife."

"I—" Her brow crinkled as she looked up at him. "I—" She broke off when he jerked his head around, the tickling in his nose finally penetrating his consciousness.

His adrenaline spiked. He swore.

The smell of the cigarette was gone. In its place was an equally distinctive smell.

Fire.

"What's wrong?"

He pushed the ring into her hand. "Get everyone away from the barn," he said calmly, though everything inside him was leaping to get *her* out of the barn. "Don't panic anyone. Just get them to move. Find Emmett Jamison." His practiced eye raced over the stalls where the horses were starting to shift nervously.

There wasn't smoke. Not yet.

But he could smell it, and knew there would be a helluva lot of it, given the fuel available.

He knew the barn wasn't wired with a sprinkler system, but that didn't explain why the alarm—which it did possess—hadn't sounded.

Bethany had closed her hand around the ring. "What—"

"Fire." He was already sliding open Barnabus' stall gate, pulling the rope halter off the hook and stepping inside with the horse. "Go, Bethany. Now."

She turned on her heel and ran around the hay maze, streaking lithely toward the wide doorway.

"Come on, boy," he murmured to the horse, sliding the halter over his head. He couldn't let the horse bolt even if the yards outside the barn hadn't been full of children. Not when horses had been known to run back into a burning barn.

From outside, he heard Bethany's voice. "Come on, everyone," she said, and even inside the barn he could hear the surprising authority in her tone. "I need you all to walk away from the barn as quickly as you can. Come on. Line up. That's it. Head across the road. Go beyond the fire engine. Toward the wall. Quickly now."

Holding Barnabus's lead rope, Darr threw Jeopardy's halter over her neck, and ran the two horses out of the barn. He handed off their halters to a stunned-looking Lorena, saw that Bethany and the other adults were rapidly rounding up the children, moving foot by foot away.

"Vane," he shouted, but he saw that the other man was already swinging up into the engine while the probie, Rick, was waving everyone away from the area.

A high scream split the air. "Look! The barn's on fire!"

Darr swore under his breath as the more-or-less orderly retreat splintered into shock. Panic was the last thing they needed. "Emmett," he yelled, spotting him. "Get those kids under control."

But the former FBI special agent who now ran the Foundation was already trotting into the melee swirling around Bethany, his voice brooking no debate as he sharply ordered everyone to keep quiet and to keep moving.

"Get these horses to the riding arena," Darr told Lorena. It was a safe distance away from the barn. "Don't let 'em run back this way." He turned back to the door.

The smoke had arrived. With a vengeance. It slunk out of the wide doorway, sneaking up toward the sky with menacing tentacles.

He ran back inside, yanking the collar of his shirt up over his nose.

Inside it was worse.

Already, fire was licking up from the corners of the hay bale maze. Even hunched low against the smoke, he could see Mojito in the last stall, prancing; could hear her groaning in agitation. "A couple minutes," he muttered, grabbing the fire extinguisher from its holster on the wall and running along the side of the smoking maze, blasting it with fire retardant as he went. "Give me a couple more minutes."

But the rear wall of the barn suddenly burst into flame. It raced hungrily upward. Outward.

Mojito threw herself against her stall door. It shuddered violently, but the gate held.

He knew Devaney would attack from the rear, but they were only half a company with an apparatus that was three decades past its prime, and the weathered barn wall was fully engulfed.

He emptied the extinguisher over the hay maze, hoping to keep the pathway clear, then ran to the stalls and the nickering horses. Climbing on the rails, he managed to lasso halters over Pasqual and Sam. Honeygirl was nearly frothing; she was almost as panicked as Mojito in the next stall. Talking all the while, he had to slip into Honeygirl's stall to reach her. He ran his hand up her quivering shoulder. She exhaled noisily, butting her head. "That's a girl," he soothed.

Three feet way, Mojito was beyond calming. Her hooves crashed against the rails again, this time slamming against those between her stall and Honeygirl's, and the wood splintered in half, catching Darr across the chest.

Honeygirl lurched, pinning him between her half ton of terrified horseflesh and the remaining rails of the stall. He grunted, gasping for breath and pushed against her hind quarters but her feet were planted. Swearing a blue streak, he smashed his fist against the rail behind his butt, and fell backwards into Mojito's when the wood gave way.

Mojito's hooves slammed down close enough to pull hair out of his head and he rolled over, shinnying back into Honeygirl's stall as Mojito reared again, barely missing him with her flying hooves. He grabbed the halter and threw it over Honeygirl's neck, bearing his weight against the lead rope to pull her unwilling soul out of the stall.

His ribs aching, he slid up on her back, laying low. "Come on, baby," he coaxed. Her ears twitched and he could feel her muscles bunching beneath him. He leaned forward and caught the edge of the latch to Sam's stall. Honeygirl nervously side-stepped. He leaned farther. Shot the latch and barely managed to grab Sam's rope before the horse could bolt.

Honeygirl whinnied. He clucked, eked another prancing side step out of her. He nearly had Pasqual's rope.

"I got him." Emmett appeared almost like an apparition out of the thick smoke, a bandanna tied around his nose. He flipped the latch open, pulled the horse out and ran ahead of Darr toward the barn doors.

Honeygirl's legs reached out, and it was all Darr could do to keep her from mowing down Emmett and Pasqual in front of them. The heat from the burning hay scorched as they streaked past the maze, but the suppressant he'd sprayed over that side was still managing to keep the fire in check.

And then they were in the clear.

He took in the sight of the children, all evaced safely away from the outbuildings. He could see Bethany, Lily and the others moving among them. Keeping them calm.

Just the sight of Bethany's blond hair and red sweater safely in the distance was enough to keep him going.

He slid off Honeygirl. Shoved the two lead ropes toward Emmett. "Mojito's still inside."

Emmett swore. "Darr, you can't go back in there."

But he would—he *had* to. The sound of the horse's cries were audible even above the roar of the fire. He grabbed a pitcher of water off the table and threw it over his shirt, yanked the shirt up over his nose and raced back through the waves of smoke billowing greedily out the door.

The visibility was nearly nil, the wet shirt clinging to his face a poor airpack. The entire top row of the maze was an open flame, reaching all the way to the roof.

He ran low. And hard. The straw on the stall floors had ignited. Jumped from there to the wood posts. The rails.

He nipped a halter off the empty stall next to Barney's before the flame could reach it, and stumbled toward Mojito.

She whinnied piteously, the sounds of her clawing hooves wrenching through him. "I'm coming, girl." He reached the last stall. The gate was smoldering; the flames behind her singeing the ends of her creamy-colored tail.

He shot his boot through the gate and the wood shattered, sparks flying. Mojito reared up and Darr grabbed her mane, yanking her down hard. Her eyes were a blind panic. He slid the halter over her fighting head, and dragged her from the stall, away from one burning wall toward another burning maze.

She reared, nearly dislocating his shoulders, but he grimly held on to the lead, pulling, dragging.

And then, just when he could see the glimmer of afternoon sun through the roiling smoke, the ground seemed to shudder around them. The horse screamed and maybe Darr did, too, as she succeeded in yanking the lead at last free from his fists, and the rear walls of the barn caved in behind them.

He lurched, fell on his knee, scrabbled forward and nearly crawled the last few feet to the barn doors.

"You're a goddamn lucky sumbitch," Devaney hollered in his ear, dragging him beneath his shoulders out into the sunshine and halfway across the field before dumping him flat on his back and leaning down into his face. "Lucky or freaking dumb." He straightened up to stomp around in a furious circle. "You got a death wish? That was a freaking *horse!*"

Darr sat up, coughing violently and doing his own cursing over the sharp pain in his ribs. There was no sign of Mojito. The horse would stop running eventually. As long as it wasn't back into the barn, Darr didn't care.

"Your hands are burned," he croaked.

"Had to play freaking hose man for a freaking incinerator!" Devaney's voice was still loud. "Had to pull back almost as soon as we hit the attack, for all the good we did. That thing went up in fifteen minutes flat."

He finally seemed to run out of steam and propped his angry red hands on his hips. Behind them, the department's new pumper had arrived, along with a water tanker, and the smoke billowing toward the sky was turning white.

But it was obvious that the barn was beyond saving.

Now it was a matter of ensuring that the fire didn't spread on the breeze to the other outbuildings or ignite the winter-dry fields, and then dealing with the cleanup.

"Helluva picnic for them." Devaney jerked his head toward the picnic-goers. "Not exactly the kind of news you Fortunes were planning to make today."

Darr looked back toward the house. Not only did it look as though every emergency rig in the county had arrived in reinforcement, but the local news truck had rolled onto the scene, as well.

He grimaced and rolled to his knees. Hugging his arm across the gnawing ache in his side, he got his feet under himself and stood.

"Where you going?"

Talking took too much effort. He waved in the general direction of the engines.

"Hell, no, you don't." Devaney hauled him back practically by his collar. "You're sitting your butt right here until a medic can check you out." He grimaced, raking his fingers through his near-white hair. "Check us both out." He stomped around in a circle some more. "How the hell'd this happen?"

Breathing was becoming a distinct hassle. "Someone was

smoking near the barn," Darr said. Which was never wise. One thoughtless flick into some greedy fuel, and the rest was history.

Fifty feet away from them, the cameraman from the news truck was practically tripping over his feet to get footage. But it was the woman running toward him, her blond hair flying behind her, that grabbed Darr's focus.

He barely managed to brace himself before Bethany flew into his outstretched arms. "Omigod." She buried her face in his neck, only to pull back, racing her gaze, her hands over him. "You're burned." Tears streaked down her cheeks.

"I'm fine."

"You can hardly speak!"

"Just the smoke." He couldn't keep from coughing.

She slipped under his shoulder, as if she fully intended to keep him from falling off his feet. "Come on. The ambulance is here."

"You gonna drag me there?"

"If I have to," she said. But her tart voice was belied by the tears.

He closed his eyes. The air was filled with smoke, and the sweet, clean smell of her hair was heaven. He would've been happy to go with her just about anywhere. "I can't leave yet. This is the Double Crown. It's family."

"And I appreciate that," Lily came up. Her face was pale, but her spine was straight. Emmett and Linda were on her heels. "But you've done enough, Darr." She pressed her lips together for a moment, obviously struggling.

He let out a rough breath and lifted his arm off Bethany's shoulder. "Fine. I've gotta report to the chief first." Still holding his side, he headed toward the command.

Bethany pressed her hand to her mouth, watching him go. She choked back a shaking breath that was terribly close to a sob.

"He's a good man." Lily ran her hand down Bethany's shoulder.

She nodded. He was the best Bethany knew.

"You stay with him," Lily added.

She managed to scrape together some composure. "What about all the children?" The buses weren't due to arrive for another hour to transport them back home, though she knew that calls were being made to hasten the process.

"We have enough volunteers on hand. We'll take care of the children. *You* take care of him." The older woman looked around. Her hair lifted in the breeze. "If he's anything like my husband was, he won't settle for anyone else."

Bethany nodded, unable to find her voice again.

"Mrs. Fortune." A helmet-haired brunette, bearing a microphone and a cameraman in her wake, approached. "Would you mind giving a statement? I've heard that the alarm system in the barn failed. Is that correct?"

Lily sighed and with a final pat on Bethany's shoulder, turned toward the news crew.

Bethany paid them absolutely no heed. She was too busy watching Darr. The second he started to make his way back from the man wearing a white fire helmet who was barking orders at everyone, she headed toward Darr, intercepting him midway between Devaney, who was fending off a raving, teary-eyed Lorena, and the news crew, and tucked herself under his arm again.

The fact that he let her take even a minimal portion of his weight told her just how much pain he had to be in. They slowly made their way toward the rear of one of the ambulances that had arrived on the heels of the fire engines.

"This seems like a weird sort of turnaround," Darr croaked, "from our first night by a fire."

"Hush. Don't try to talk."

"You're wearing my ring."

Her fist curled. She couldn't even remember exactly when she'd pushed it onto her finger after he'd sent her running out of the barn. "Yes."

"Is that a *yes* yes?"

She pressed her lips together for a moment. "Yes." There wasn't any other answer. Not since she'd felt her heart nearly stop at the sight of him racing in and out of that barn. "Now stop talking because listening to you is making *my* throat hurt."

"You're gonna be one bossy wife," he muttered, but even through the soot and grime caked on his face, she could see the flash of his dimple.

Wife.

She swallowed hard and turned to the white-shirted EMT. "He's burned. And something's wrong with his ribs."

"Don't worry, ma'am. We've got him."

She nodded and moved back as the man helped Darr up and through the rear doors. "I'll follow in your truck to the hospital." She'd driven it to the ranch since Darr had arrived with the engine and the rest of their crew.

Darr nodded, and lifted his hand. His blue eyes looked at her above the small oxygen mask the EMT gave him.

And then the door closed, and she stood there, watching the ambulance slowly nose its way back through the throng.

Chapter Twelve

"Come on, honey," Lorena said from behind her. The ambulance was long gone. "I'll ride with you over to the hospital."

Bethany brushed her hands over her wet cheeks and turned. "Thanks."

Lorena closed the last few feet between them, lifting a shoulder. "Nobody said it's easy loving a firefighter. We need all the support we can get."

Bethany looked past the other woman. She could see no sign of Devaney, however. Just a mass of confusion as the Jamisons and Lily and the rest of the adults dealt with getting the children organized. "How long have—"

"As long as I can remember," Lorena sighed. "I keep looking for someone else." She shook her head. "Problem is, nobody else is *him*." She looped her arm through Bethany's. "The cursed fool." She nearly spit. Then laughed brokenly.

This time, it was Bethany who squeezed Lorena's hand. "Darr's truck is up by the house."

It was nearly two frustrating hours before Bethany could maneuver the big vehicle around and through the blocked roads and turn through the main gate of the Double Crown to head back to town. Lorena was true to her word, not leaving Bethany's side until they reached the emergency room at the hospital where the attendant had clearly been ordered by Darr to send his fiancée immediately back to him.

"I'll wait here," Lorena told Bethany, and gestured at the molded plastic seats in the waiting room. "I want to know he's okay, too. You go on back."

Needing no further urging, Bethany went through the double doors. Darr was in the first bed, right around the corner.

His face was marginally cleaner, though a thin oxygen tube stretched from his nose to the unit affixed to the wall beside the bed.

The charred T-shirt had been removed from his wide shoulders and he was holding an ice pack against his side, but it did nothing to hide the scrapes and angry red splotches dotting his arms and shoulders.

Even his turnout pants were gone, leaving only his blue jeans in place.

"Hello, again." Dr. Waite looked over Darr's chart when Bethany stopped next to his bed. "Seems like nothing but excitement for the two of you." He scratched on the chart. "Nurse'll be by soon to dress your cuts and those burns," he told Darr. "From what I hear, you're lucky they're not worse."

"I'm lucky all right." Darr slid his hand around hers. His fingers toyed with the ring that was slightly loose around her finger. "How quick can I get out of here?"

"Still waiting on the films we took when you arrived.

Whether there are fractures are not, you've got some seriously nasty contusions. You're going to be black and blue and every other color of the rainbow before long. I want to keep you until morning for observation."

"No." Darr immediately shook his head.

Dr. Waite's lips twisted. "Of all people, you ought to know better, Darr. The FD takes a dim view of its employees—particularly a paramedic who knows better—leaving AMA after an incident."

Darr grimaced. "You're not moving me to a regular room."

"Then as long as we don't need the bed, you can stay in here," Dr. Waite countered immediately. He glanced at the clock on the wall. "And if you don't keep that oxygen in place, it might well be tomorrow night before I spring you." He tapped the side of the chart on the end of Darr's bed and strode away.

"Control freak," Darr muttered after the departing doctor.

"It's just until morning," Bethany soothed.

He made a low, impatient sound. But when he patted the bed beside him, his smoke-charred voice was anything but impatient. "Sit here." He waited until she'd stretched her hip up onto the high bed. "Are you okay?"

She exhaled. "*You're* the one laying in the E.R. this time."

"Yeah, but stress isn't good for the baby."

He rubbed his hand over her abdomen and she suspected the immediate bump inside her wasn't just a coincidence.

"Have you thought of any better names?"

She leaned down and carefully avoiding brushing against his poor, battered chest, then pressed her lips to his. "I've already told you. *Darr.* If that's too horrible for you to contemplate, then we'll call him DJ for Darr Junior."

"Ah-hem." A deep male voice interrupted them. "Sorry to

interrupt," Nick said, looking anything but. "I had to find out on the evening news that my baby brother was here!"

"I would'a called," Darr defended.

"Yeah. Once you were home and snug in your jammies." Nick crossed his arms, eyeing them with clear displeasure that didn't do a thing to mask his concern. "Look, I know I opened my mouth when I shouldn't have, but have either one of you ever heard of a *phone* call?"

Bethany slid off the bed. She'd have called the man herself if she'd known how to reach him, but judging from his expression, she doubted he wanted to hear excuses.

"You two can hash this out. Lorena's in the waiting room," she told Darr. "She wanted to know that you're all right."

Darr reluctantly let go of her hand and watched her walk away.

"I see she's wearing Grandma's ring," Nick said the second she disappeared through the swinging doors.

"I told you I was going to marry her."

"Yeah, well, I didn't know she'd agreed. You've been together what? Two weeks? This is insanity, Darr. Even you've got to see that."

"The only insanity is not marrying the woman I love," he said, coughing through his clenched teeth. "Maybe if you've ever really loved someone, you'd know that."

Nick sighed noisily. "I'm not bashing Barbara," he said. "She seems perfectly nice." His gaze was sober. "I'm just not convinced you're not trying for a Celia do-over."

Darr dropped his wrist over his eyes. God. He was tired.

But Nick wasn't finished. "How d'you know you're not just replacing her? Christ man, you couldn't have found a woman more identical if you'd tried."

"Celia's dead," Darr said wearily. "Just because Bethany's pregnant doesn't mean I'm confusing the two of them."

"Bethany?"

Dammit. "Barbara."

"Well which is it?"

"It's Bethany." Her voice startled them both.

Darr dropped his arm. Pain—inside, outside—dredged through him.

She was standing just inside the swinging doors. Her face was pale. She continued forward to set a bottle of water on the rolling table beside Darr. "The nurse asked me to bring that to you." Her voice was brittle.

"Beth—"

But she was already focusing on Nick. "My name is Bethany Burdett. If you do an Internet search, you might find a few scandalous notes about how I ran out on the day of my wedding. But unless you already knew that, I doubt that's the similarity between me and Darr's Celia that you find so objectionable."

"She wasn't *mine*," Darr said, but neither Bethany nor his brother was listening.

"You're not objectionable," Nick apologized. "I never meant to imply that you were. I just don't want to see Darr rushing into something for the wrong reasons. It's not fair to either one of you!"

Darr could feel his temper rising. "I grew outta short pants a long time ago, Nick. And I can judge for myself what's fair or not."

"You're absolutely right." Bethany's chin lifted as she faced Nick head-on. "Rushing into something—particularly a marriage—for the wrong reasons isn't good. Neither is tip-toeing your way into one when the reasons are all wrong. And guess what? I've tried both ways."

She slid the ring off her finger and set it beside the water bottle.

Darr jackknifed up again, grunted against the pain that made his head swim and his stomach revolt. "Wait—"

"Wrong reasons," Bethany said, her voice thick. "What if all of it's been for the wrong reason?" Her glistening gaze turned back to Darr.

He reached for her, but she was too far away. "I never loved Celia," he said evenly. "Never. And maybe if I'd have tried harder, I could have kept her from going back again to the guy who beat the life out of her and the baby of his she was carrying. Or maybe not. Because she didn't love me, either.

"I love *you.* That's my only reason. Baby. No baby. Bethany. Barbara. *It doesn't matter to me.* I want a life with you. A future." A cough racked through him. "So the question that leaves is whether or not you love me!"

A tear slid down her cheek. "I do." She bit her lip. Swiped her hand over her cheek. "But what if the reason I feel that way is only because when I'm with *you,* I'm not afraid? I'm sorry." Her voice went hoarse. "Maybe that just makes me like Celia, after all."

She turned on her heel and plunged through the doors.

Darr stared after her, frozen for only a moment before he tore the oxygen tube off and tossed it aside.

Just turning enough to slide his boots off the side of the bed prompted a new symphony of pain to swell inside him. "Move out of my way," he warned Nick, who was still standing there, looking grimly subdued.

Nick hesitated.

Darr glared.

"Here." His brother pulled off his wool coat and handed it to Darr. "You can't go running after her without a shirt."

He could. But he took the long coat, anyway. And alternately cursing and coughing, with Nick's help he managed to slide off the bed onto his own feet, and work his arms into the coat.

Nick took the water bottle and pushed it into Darr's hands. "I'll drive."

"Oh, yeah. *Now* you decide to be helpful." He grabbed his grandmother's ring and pushed through the double doors, nearly mowing down a young nurse who was coming from the opposite direction, a plastic cart of dressings in her hand. "Sorry."

"Lt. Fortune! Where do you think you're going?" She scurried after them. "I don't think Dr. Waite wants you to leave—"

The glass doors slid open and Darr strode through, leaving behind the nurse's alarmed admonitions.

"Over there." Nick gestured toward his Porsche. It was illegally parked in the red zone.

There was no sign of Darr's truck. Which meant that, despite what she'd said, Bethany had chosen to use it.

All the quicker to get away from him.

Nick beeped open the locks and Darr pulled the passenger door open and eyed the low, *low* seat. This was gonna hurt.

There was no grace or finesse involved in the act, but he managed to flop his body down into the car. His teeth were still grinding together over the oaths congested in his throat when Nick drove out of the parking lot.

"Your place?" he asked.

Would Bethany go to the apartment?

He doubted it. Not now.

"Bethany's."

Silently, Nick pulled a U-turn in the middle of the intersection, blithely ignoring the tooting horns he earned, and headed in the other direction. "I suppose karma's going to bite me on the ass for all this."

Darr still had a strong desire to kick his brother in that very spot. "No, but some day…somewhere…there's going to be a woman who knocks you on your ass." He leaned his head back against the seat, breathing very carefully. "And I'm going to sit back and love every—" he searched for a suitable word "—tormented minute she causes you."

"You never could stay mad at anyone for long." The corner of Nick's lip kicked up as he shot him a look before turning through the neighborhood leading to Bethany's street.

Darr could deal with anything that Nick said to him.

What he couldn't tolerate was Bethany getting hurt in the process.

She loved him. He knew she did.

"Drive faster," he told Nick.

The powerful car obligingly leapt forward.

"What are you going to do if she's not there?" Gravel spun beneath Nick's wheels as he turned and flew past John Decker's place and gunned up the hill.

"Find her."

"Where else would she—holy mother." Nick leaned forward, spotting the sight of the helicopter sitting at the top of the hill at the same time Darr did. "You've gotta be kidding me. Bailey-Burdett? She's one of *those* Burdetts?"

Darr eyed the name plastered on the side of the silver bird and swore inside. "So?" He couldn't care less what Burdetts she belonged to. He was a lot more interested in getting to Bethany.

His truck was parked at an angle next to the porch steps. The front door was open.

Beside him, Nick shook his head dolefully. He pulled the car to a stop near the truck and pushed open his door. "Bailey-Burdett is only one of the largest private oil companies left."

He made it around to Darr's side before he could even

manage to heave himself out of the low seat. He grabbed Darr's arms and pulled him up.

Darr wheezed. Hell. "In Texas?"

"In…anywhere. You do *not* look good."

Darr pushed past his brother and made it to the steps. He grabbed the cold, metal railing and grimly planted his heavy boot on the first step.

"—house is an embarrassment, Bethany Ann." A shrill female voice floated out the door. "What were you thinking?"

"I was thinking I was glad to find it because the rent was cheap." Bethany's voice was dull.

Darr pulled himself up the second step.

"Cheap! It's a dump. How could you do this to us? We even had to hear from Charlotte Myers—who is the *biggest* gossip in Dallas—that she saw you on the news tonight. Lyle and your father and I manage to convince all our friends that you're recuperating in the Caribbean, and *you* go and get yourself on the news, looking like some… Orphan Annie!

He made the third step. Impatiently waved off Nick behind him.

"Sorry, Mother, but I just couldn't fit in a trip to the spa when there was fire burning around our ears."

"Do you have any idea of the effort it took to find out where you were living? The favors your father had to call in? Can you imagine his embarrassment when we discovered you weren't even using your own name? And *this* is what we find when we get here? A hovel that's falling down around your ears! Honestly. I just don't know what to say to you. Stuart, *you* talk to your daughter."

"Now, Angela, don't upset yourself."

Darr stepped into the doorway, taking in the tableau.

Bethany, shoulders hunched and hugging her arms around herself, faced off against the other three.

Her father. Her mother—who seemed to find plenty to say as far as Darr was concerned.

And the tall, tight-lipped jerk who was undoubtedly Lyle.

Darr braced his feet in the doorway. "I'd rather you not *upset* my fiancée."

Bethany whirled. Her heart very nearly stopped in her chest at the sight of Darr standing stalwart in her doorway. "What are you doing here?"

"Fiancée!" Bethany's mother lifted her carefully arranged head right up from her gray-haired husband's shoulder at that. Considering all the noisy sobbing she was doing, her makeup had managed to remain impeccable.

"She's all but my wife," Lyle snapped. "I've got a license that only needs signing."

Darr slanted a look toward the man. "Is that a fact?" His voice was even.

Ignoring them all, Bethany took a step toward him, her hands lifting, only to pull back and hug her waist again. "You're supposed to be at the hospital."

"There, we're in agreement," Nick said from behind.

"What kind of circus *is* this?" Angela's voice rose again. "Bethany, I demand to know who these people are!"

Bethany closed her eyes, pressing her fingertips to the pain in her forehead that had been there since she'd arrived at the house only to find her father's helicopter parked in the road, and her worst nightmares standing in the center of her little house as if they were afraid to touch any of the old, simple furniture.

"Angela, be quiet," Stuart ordered, and mercifully, Angela subsided. "Bethany, we're leaving at once. Lyle's been very patient with your nonsense, but enough is enough. Now he's agreed to a quiet ceremony in Judge Dooley's chambers the moment we land in Dall—"

"Recuperating from what?" She interrupted, dropping her hand to eye her mother. "You convinced everyone that I was recuperating. From *what?*"

"Don't take that tone with me." Angela sniffed, looking the picture of wounded motherhood.

"Painkillers," Lyle inserted.

Bethany blinked. "Excuse me?"

"It was a plausible excuse," Angela defended, "to explain away your appalling behavior. Now, as your father was saying, Judge Dooley can perform the ceremony as soon as we arrive back home. We'll make the wedding announcement while you and Lyle go somewhere. Observe at least a brief honeymoon."

"You'd rather everyone think your daughter is hooked on painkillers than that she had the sense to keep from marrying the man you virtually sold her to?" She waved her hand dismissively toward Lyle.

"Sold? Bethany, don't be ridiculous." Lyle reached his hand out toward her.

"Put that hand on her and I'll break it off," Darr said in a low voice.

But Bethany wasn't worried about Lyle. He was beneath contempt and had been all along.

She stepped closer to her father. "Sold," she repeated tightly. "How else would you describe your arrangement with him?"

Stuart's lips thinned. "Nothing more than a business agreement. Don't be naive, Bethany. Bailey-Burdett needs capital and Lyle has it."

"But he was only willing to give it in exchange for me. It didn't matter to you that he had a little problem controlling his *fists*. The only thing *you* cared about was the money!"

"Do you want us to start laying people off, Bethany? Do you want to know that our employees are losing their houses, their cars, all because you won't do your duty for the family?"

"And what about your duty as a parent to me?" She shook her head. Her hand rested on the mound of her child. Her son.

Realization was swelling through her and it was heady. "You know, I was terrified of this moment. Of you finding me. Coming with that almighty confidence that I'd do your bidding. After all, until the wedding, I'd always done just that." She eyed her mother. "I wore my hair the way you wanted. Dressed the way you wanted. Joined the clubs, dated the boys, took the classes. I even agreed to marry a man I knew I didn't love because it was what *you* wanted. I wasn't smart like Bailey or Julia. All I had going for me were my looks. And the connections you made sure I made."

Angela huffed. "And what's wrong with that? Lyle can give you everything you've ever wanted."

"No, Mother." Her lips compressed. "Lyle can give you and Daddy everything *you've* ever wanted." She lifted her chin. "I hope you'll all be very happy together. But for me? We're done."

"What's that supposed to mean?"

Bethany drew herself up to her full height. "Well, Daddy, it means that you're standing in my house and I'm telling all of you to leave."

Her mother looked truly appalled. "But Lyle—"

"But Lyle nothing. He can take his money and buy himself another compliant little bride. And God have mercy on her if she doesn't see through him more quickly than I did."

Lyle's eyes narrowed coldly. "You really are a stupid little bi—"

"You're getting on my nerves," Darr warned.

"And you really are a pathetic excuse of a man, Lyle," Bethany returned evenly.

"Bethany." Stuart took her shoulders. "The last few months have been hard on us all. Try to see reason. The capital we need—"

"How much?" Darr asked suddenly.

"How much what?"

"How much money?" Nick leaned over Darr's shoulder. His smile was as icy as Darr's unsmiling expression.

Stuart glared. "Who *are* you?"

"Darr Fortune."

"I'm his brother. Nick. Fortune, that'd be."

Angela's expression perked. "*The* Fortunes?"

"Get out!" Bethany shouted.

Her mother's jaw dropped inelegantly. "You can't kick us out. We're your parents, for heaven's sake."

"I can. And I am." She pushed her father's hands off her shoulder. "I'll sign over Grandmother's trust to you, Daddy. You can do whatever you want with it. I don't care."

Angela swept her with a wounded look. "Easy to say now that you've got a Fortune on the hook."

Bethany couldn't bring herself to look at Darr. She'd been so afraid of making the wrong decision as far as he was concerned, and that's *exactly* what she'd done by leaving his side for even one moment. "*Out.*"

Angela snatched up her fur coat and swung it around her shoulders. "You're an ungrateful, ungrateful child."

"I'm not ungrateful at all, Mother." She patted her abdomen. "You've taught me everything I need to know about what not to do as a parent."

Angela swept past Darr, who'd obligingly shifted out of the doorway.

"This isn't what I wanted, Bethany." Her father stared down at her. She liked to think there was regret in his blue eyes, but knew if there was, it was probably because her grandmother's trust—though substantial—was still merely a fraction of the investment Lyle had agreed to make upon their "I do's."

"It isn't what I wanted, either."

"What will you do?"

"Live my life," she said simply.

His lips pressed together. After a moment, he gave one short nod, and followed after his wife.

"Don't think you're going to get support out of me for that baby." Lyle remained behind. "It's probably not even mine."

"He's not."

He snorted. "Right. You're a cold little fish in bed. If I hadn't wanted to get into Bailey-Burdett so badly, I'd have gotten rid of you after Switzerland. Whose else would it be?"

Bethany looked over at Darr. "His," she said.

Lyle's eyes glinted furiously. "I should have known you were a whore the first—"

"That's it." Darr's fist connected and Lyle's head snapped back.

Bethany gasped and darted forward, even as Lyle straightened, his fists curling. A bead of blood trailed from the corner of his split lip.

She wrapped her hands around Darr's inflexible arm. "He's not worth it, Darr."

Darr didn't blink.

Anger vibrated from Lyle's pores. He faced down Darr for an interminable moment.

"You really want to try?" Darr asked softly.

Lyle's gaze slid from Darr to Nick standing right behind

him. Finally, with a grimace, he turned on his heel and stomped past both of the fierce Fortunes, wiping his bloody lip on his finger.

Bethany realized she was still squeezing Darr's arm. She let go. Folded her arms together. Looked away.

"Think I'll make sure he doesn't get lost on the way to the helicopter," Nick said into the thick silence. He closed the door behind him.

Bethany chewed her lip. Inside, she was shaking. "I'm sorry. They were here when I got to the house. I…I never wanted you to see what they were like. What…I…was like." Her throat tightened with the sudden tears that rose.

"What *you* are is brave. And beautiful."

"I was foolish," she said. Her chest ached. "I had you. And I—I just walked away."

"You still have me."

"You deserve someone so much better than me."

He slid his hands around her face, until she could see nothing but him. His strong face. His steady, steady blue eyes. "I deserve a woman who loves me. Who'll lie with me and laugh with me and fight with me over what—" his voice broke "—what to name our kids."

"People are going to think you're crazy, you know. When they learn I'm not Barbara Burton."

"Barbara Burton is just a name." His smoke-roughened voice slid over her as softly as his thumb stroking over her jaw. "You were never anyone but yourself. And who cares what anyone else thinks? We know what matters."

"But I gave you back your ring." She wanted to wail.

"We can take care of that." He reached into his pocket, wincing at the movement.

"Darr." She wanted to touch him, but was afraid if she did,

she'd cause him more pain. "You need to get back to the hospital. I'll get Nick—"

"I have a cracked rib. Maybe two." He coughed slightly. "Three. But first things…first." He lifted her left hand. Held the ring. "Do you promise to keep it on this time? If you're scared, bothered, whatever. You'll talk to me instead of walking away?"

"I am scared," she admitted. The words felt raw. "I'm scared that you'll realize I'm not what you deserve."

He slid the ring over fingertip. "I'm scared you'll decide I'm not what *you* deserve. I'm a firefighter, Bethany. You've seen what I do."

She pushed her finger the rest of the way through the ring. "I've seen who you are." Tears slid down her face as she leaned toward him. "And I'll never take it off again. I do love you."

"And I love you." His arm slid around her shoulders, pulling her closer, whether the action hurt or not. "Both of you," he promised, sealing his mouth over hers.

When he finally lifted his head, she was the one who was swaying.

"We *are* going to talk about this name business, though," he said. "DJ? I've got a brother who's JR. I used to call him Alphabet Soup."

She slipped her fingers through his hair. It was sooty and singed. If the speed of the last few weeks was any indication, she'd better learn not to blink too much or she might miss something. And she fully intended to savor ever minute of her life with this man. "We'll discuss it," she promised. "On the way to the hospital."

"There's that bossy thing again." He grinned. Wry. Sexy. Wonderful. "Turns me on."

She couldn't help laughing, though her wet cheeks went hot. "*You* are dangerous."

He lifted her hand to his mouth. Kissed her knuckles. "No. I'm just yours."

The truth of it was filling her soul. And it was glorious.

She pulled open the door. "And I am yours." And leaning on each other, they headed out into their future.

Epilogue

"Your face is looking a lot better than the last time I saw you, Darr." Lily Fortune tilted her head around the opened doorway to Darr's hospital room. "Mind if I come in?"

It was two days since the fire at the Double Crown. Two days since Bethany had sent her parents and Lyle packing in that helicopter that ended up being the talk of the town. Two days since Darr had put his grandmother's ring on Bethany's finger.

For a second time.

This time, he knew it was staying there.

"Join the party." He gestured Lily into the room that was crowded with people. Devaney with his arm looped around Lorena's shoulders. Rick and his girlfriend, Elise. Marcus and Joe and their wives.

SusieMae was also there, having brought a huge platter of barbecue ribs and coleslaw, because—as she'd claimed—the hospital food was worse than rat food. Even John Decker, nearly up to his elbows in the ribs, was proof that SusieMae's food was delicious.

Lily's smile widened and she slipped into the room, looking around for some place to set the tall, leafy-green plant she'd brought.

"I can take that." Bethany slid off Darr's bedside and reached for the plant. "There's some room left on the windowsill." It was already crowded with stuff that his visitors seemed compelled to bring. Plastic fire trucks with yellow flowers blooming out the top, balloons, black roses—Devaney's idea of humor, naturally.

"Thank you, dear." Lily leaned down and bussed Bethany's cheek. When she straightened again, her gaze narrowed slightly. "I have to say, you just look lovelier than ever."

Bethany blushed, dashing her hand down the front of her pink blouse. "Thank you."

Lily caught Bethany's hand, holding the ring up for her inspection. "Ah. So *this* is why there's an extra glow." Looking delighted, she scooted past Devaney to lean over Darr and gently hug him, too. "When's the date?"

"Knowing those two, about five minutes from now," Nick deadpanned from his position leaning against one wall. "Afraid if I blink, I'll miss out on best-man duties."

"We haven't set the date yet," Darr said over the laughter Nick earned. His fingers looped through Bethany's after she'd rearranged the windowsill and resumed her spot next to him on the bed.

Her clear blue gaze met his and in them he saw forever. "Don't worry, though," he assured. "We'll keep you posted."

"Well," Lily said. "I do love a wedding. And they always seem to come in batches. Jane and Jorge. The two of you." She smiled again. "I don't want to bother you for long. I just wanted to drop by and thank you again." Her hand waved to encompass the others. "Thank all of you, for everything you did at the Double Crown. If you hadn't been there, I don't know what might have happened."

Darr managed to tear himself out of the depths of his future bride's eyes. "This is two too many fires we've had around here. I should've chased off the idiot who was smoking when I noticed the smell."

"That is not your fault," Lily said emphatically. "There are No Smoking signs posted all over. I just blame myself for not having the alarm system checked before the picnic."

"The alarm might have bought us a few minutes," Devaney said. "But the barn was prime fuel. I don't think anything would've saved it, Miz Fortune."

"At least we got the horses out," Darr said. "Mojito still hasn't turned up yet?"

Lily shook her head. "We're looking."

Bethany's hand stroked his shoulder. "Well." He let out a sigh and focused on something he could do something about. "If you need help cleaning up out there, just call—"

"You?" Lily's eyebrows rose with sudden amusement as she looked over his bandage-bound chest.

"Devaney," Darr finished.

Devaney snorted. "Guy cracks a couple 'a ribs and thinks he can get outta all the hard work. You're going to fit right in with the higher-ups, when you make cap'n."

Her throat felt tight, but Lily managed to keep the smile on her face, as the lively bunch teased Darr. "I've got the ranch taken care of," she assured them. For the first time in a long while, though, her confidence about that fact was starting to crack. "Now, I'll leave you in Bethany's good hands."

It was plainly obvious to her that no matter how recently they'd found each other, those two were meant to be.

It was so easy to remember Ryan looking at her the way Darr looked at Bethany. So easy to remember how she'd felt looking back at him.

She turned to leave, but Nick had pushed away from his loner position against the wall. "I'll walk you to your car."

"Darling, that's not necessary." She shooed him back toward the room. "Stay. Enjoy yourself."

Behind his glasses, Nick's brown gaze was sharp. "Are you sure you're all right?"

She patted his cheek. "Of course."

His brows twitched together. But after a moment, he nodded. "Okay." He leaned down and dropped a kiss on her cheek. "Anytime you want to deal some poker, you let me know." His grin was quick and Fortune-handsome.

She kept her smile in place until she was well away from Darr's private room and the revelry that followed her footsteps down the corridor.

But in her pocket burned the note she'd found after the fire. The note that proved it hadn't been a carelessly discarded cigarette that had caused it.

The note that said, *This one wasn't an accident, either.*

Despite the crowd in his room, Darr eyed Nick when he returned. He could see something unsettled in his brother's eyes. "Everything alright?"

"Just a little poker talk," Nick assured with a smooth smile.

"Poker?" Bethany's soft hair brushed Darr's jaw as her head turned. "I like to play poker."

"No kidding." Nick eyed her, obviously considering.

"Forget it," Darr warned. "If she's anything like she is at Monopoly, she's a shark."

"Hey." Bethany shot him an amused look.

"A beautiful shark," he revised, unable to resist running his fingers through her hair even if there were a half dozen people around to witness it.

Her blue eyes darkened, going from amused to slumberous in less than a blink. "That's a little better, I suppose."

He suddenly wanted his half dozen visitors gone in the worst way. "You know, I...I appreciate everyone coming, but I'm bushed," he said loudly. "I think I need some sleep."

Bethany immediately began to sit up and away from him. "Of course you're tired. This has probably been exhausting for you."

Darr slid his hand up the back of her soft blouse and closed his fingers right over the stretchy waistband of her pants, holding her in place where no one could see. He ignored the startled look she cast him and accepted the knuckle knocks and the careful hugs and kisses he got as the rest of the group began their noisy exodus.

Nick was the last to go. "*Sleepy* my aunt Fanny," he drawled knowingly as he pulled the door closed.

And then there was nothing but blessed silence as Darr looked at Bethany. "See if the door locks."

Her lips rounded. She slowly shook her head. "No. Oh, no. We can't." But her gaze still slid tellingly toward the door. "You're hurt, for heaven's sake!"

"And there's nothing more healing than your touch." His hand drifted from the back of her waistband to the front, spreading across her abdomen.

She exhaled, trying to look disapproving and failing miserably, judging by the faint smile that lurked around her soft lips. "How can you possibly think about...that...when you're all battered and bruised?"

"Lock the door and I'll be happy to explain."

A short, soft laugh escaped her. But she slid off the bed and went to the door. "It does have a lock." She sounded surprised.

For that matter, he was a little surprised, too.

And grateful as all get-out, particularly when, after a quick glance at him, she turned it. Then she leaned back against the door, looking at him from across the room. "We really shouldn't."

"Oh, I think we really should." He lifted his hand, beckoning.

Her head tilted slightly. Her lips twitched. "Are the rest of our lives going to be like this, Darwin Fortune? You crook your finger and I come running?"

"It only seems fair, Bethany soon-to-be-Fortune. You're on this earth and I come running."

Her eyes softened. "What am I going to do with you?"

"Love me," he said seriously.

She slowly pushed away from the door. "Oh, Darr. That I will always do." She carefully lifted her hip onto the bed beside him and leaned over him. "I love you." Her words whispered against his lips. "Now—" her hand trailed lightly down his chest, over the hospital-issue gown he'd been protesting since the nurses had practically strapped it around him "—tomorrow—" she reached the sheet bunched around his waist "—always."

He caught her slender fingers when they crept beneath the sheet. "What about all that *we can't* business?"

She managed to slide beneath the sheet while he was still busy falling headlong into her sweetly sexy, slow smile. "A good fiancée is going to do whatever she can to see that her future husband heals as quickly as possible. After all—" she settled, light as a feather, over him "—we have a wedding date to set."

His throat felt more than a little tight. "Yeah. We can do that."

"Yes." She pressed her lips to his again. "We can."

And they did.

HARLEQUIN® *Romance.*

This February the Harlequin® Romance series
will feature six Diamond Brides stories featuring
diamond proposals and gorgeous grooms.

Share your dream wedding proposal and you could WIN!

The most romantic entry will win a diamond
necklace and will inspire a proposal in one of
our upcoming Diamond Grooms books in 2010.

In 100 words or less, tell us the most romantic
way that you dream of being proposed to.

For more information, and to enter
the Diamond Brides Proposal contest, please visit
www.DiamondBridesProposal.com

Or mail your entry to us at:
IN THE U.S.: 3010 Walden Ave., P.O. Box 9069, Buffalo, NY 14269-9069
IN CANADA: 225 Duncan Mill Road, Don Mills, ON M3B 3K9

www.eHarlequin.com   HRCONTESTFEB09

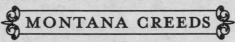

REQUEST YOUR FREE BOOKS!

2 FREE NOVELS PLUS 2 FREE GIFTS!

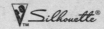

SPECIAL EDITION®

Life, Love and Family!

YES! Please send me 2 FREE Silhouette Special Edition® novels and my 2 FREE gifts (gifts are worth about $10). After receiving them, if I don't wish to receive any more books, I can return the shipping statement marked "cancel." If I don't cancel, I will receive 6 brand-new novels every month and be billed just $4.24 per book in the U.S. or $4.99 per book in Canada, plus 25¢ shipping and handling per book and applicable taxes, if any*. That's a savings of at least 15% off the cover price! I understand that accepting the 2 free books and gifts places me under no obligation to buy anything. I can always return a shipment and cancel at any time. Even if I never buy another book from Silhouette, the two free books and gifts are mine to keep forever.

235 SDN EEYU   335 SDN EEY6

Name	(PLEASE PRINT)

Address	Apt. #

City	State/Prov.	Zip/Postal Code

Signature (if under 18, a parent or guardian must sign)

Mail to the **Silhouette Reader Service:**
IN U.S.A.: P.O. Box 1867, Buffalo, NY 14240-1867
IN CANADA: P.O. Box 609, Fort Erie, Ontario L2A 5X3

Not valid to current subscribers of Silhouette Special Edition books.

Want to try two free books from another line?
Call 1-800-873-8635 or visit www.morefreebooks.com.

* Terms and prices subject to change without notice. N.Y. residents add applicable sales tax. Canadian residents will be charged applicable provincial taxes and GST. Offer not valid in Quebec. This offer is limited to one order per household. All orders subject to approval. Credit or debit balances in a customer's account(s) may be offset by any other outstanding balance owed by or to the customer. Please allow 4 to 6 weeks for delivery. Offer available while quantities last.

Your Privacy: Silhouette is committed to protecting your privacy. Our Privacy Policy is available online at www.eHarlequin.com or upon request from the Reader Service. From time to time we make our lists of customers available to reputable third parties who may have a product or service of interest to you. If you would prefer we not share your name and address, please check here. ☐

SSE08R

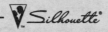

SPECIAL EDITION

TRAVIS'S APPEAL

by *USA TODAY* bestselling author
MARIE FERRARELLA

Shana O'Reilly couldn't deny it—family lawyer
Travis Marlowe had some kind of appeal. But
as Travis handled her father's tricky estate
planning, he discovered things weren't what
they seemed in the O'Reilly clan. Would
an explosive secret leave Travis and Shana's
budding relationship in tatters?

*Available March 2009
wherever books are sold.*

The Inside Romance newsletter has a NEW look for the new year!

Same great content, brand-new look!

The Inside Romance newsletter is a FREE quarterly newsletter highlighting our upcoming series releases and promotions!

Click on the Inside Romance link on the front page of **www.eHarlequin.com** or e-mail us at insideromance@harlequin.ca to sign up to receive your FREE newsletter today!

You can also subscribe by writing to us at: HARLEQUIN BOOKS Attention: Customer Service Department P.O. Box 9057, Buffalo, NY 14269-9057

Please allow 4-6 weeks for delivery of the first issue by mail.

IRNNEW09

You're invited to join our Tell Harlequin Reader Panel!

By joining our new reader panel you will:

- Receive Harlequin® books—they are FREE and yours to keep with no obligation to purchase anything!
- Participate in fun online surveys
- Exchange opinions and ideas with women just like you
- Have a say in our new book ideas and help us publish the best in women's fiction

In addition, you will have a chance to win great prizes and receive special gifts! See Web site for details. Some conditions apply. Space is limited.

To join, visit us at
www.TellHarlequin.com.

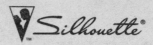
Silhouette®

SSECNMBPA0209